Father
Brother
Keeper

Stories ———————————

Nathan Poole

Winner of the 2013 Mary McCarthy Prize in Short Fiction
Selected by Edith Pearlman

Sarabande  Books

LOUISVILLE, KENTUCKY

Managing Editor
Sarabande Books, Inc.
2234 Dundee Road, Suite 200
Louisville, KY 40205

Library of Congress Cataloging-in-Publication Data

Poole, Nathan.
  Father brother keeper : stories / Nathan Poole. -- First edition.
    pages cm
    Summary: "Winner of the 2013 Mary McCarthy Prize in Short Fiction Selected by Edith Pearlman"—Provided by publisher.
  ISBN 978-1-936747-94-8 (paperback)
  1. Southern States—Social life and customs—Fiction. I. Title.
  PS3616.O6375F38 2015
  813'.6—dc23

2014010435

Cover artwork: "Bottom Creek, Bent Mountain, VA" by Genesis Chapman. Ink on yupo paper. Provided by the artist. genesischapman.com

Cover and interior layout by Kirkby Gann Tittle.

Manufactured in Canada.

This book is printed on acid-free paper.

Sarabande Books is a nonprofit literary organization.

amazon.com.

This project is supported in part by an award from the National Endowment for the Arts.

The Kentucky Arts Council, the state arts agency, supports Sarabande Books with state tax dollars and federal funding from the National Endowment for the Arts.

To Octama, James, and Mildred

I am moved by fancies that are curled
Around these images, and cling:
The notion of some infinitely gentle
Infinitely suffering thing.

—T. S. Eliot

Contents

Foreword by Edith Pearlman | *vii*

A Map of the Watershed | *3*

Fallow Dog | *27*

The Strength of Fields | *46*

Stretch Out Your Hand | *58*

Two From Sparta:

1. Anchor Tree Passing | *74*

2. Silas | *86*

Lipochrome | *97*

The Firelighter | *113*

Year of the Champion Trees | *135*

They Were Calling to One Another | *154*

Swing Low Sweet Chicken Baby | *166*

Father Brother Keeper | *173*

Acknowledgments | *197*

The Author | *199*

Foreword

One of the many things good fiction can do is to teach us something new about the world. Another is to exercise the possibilities of language. *Father Brother Keeper* does both. Many of these stories are set in rural Georgia. "Rotund fields rising and falling away in succession—appeared like conquered giants, like slain things left on their backs in the sun, showing their swollen and furrowed underbellies." This description of mauled nature prefigures later descriptions. The stories in this book are linked not only by place but more tellingly by images that repeat with variation.

In another tale a little girl dies from raw milk fever. Her six bereaved brothers sit side by side outside the cabin, "the youngest tearing a leaf in half and throwing the strips out behind his legs" in the mindless way of the grief-stricken. Other stories reflect this talented author's habit of looking closely and thinking deeply. A girl is transfixed by her fear of horses; a family is frozen by the father's madness; a child stricken by her parents' split tears her clothes to shreds.

Besides showing us place and work directly, and instructing us subtly about emotion and memory, fiction, and especially short fiction, can deliver a surprise that changes both character's and reader's perception of events. The character and the reader become briefly one. "Fallow Dog" begins with the protagonist's discovery of bait dogs on his property. Bait dogs, we learn and intuit, chained, are used to train fighter dogs to fight and kill. Having come to the end of their unspeakable careers, these dogs have been left to die. Their moribund condition is rendered in simple prose used to devastating effect. Of a mastiff: "the right side of its mouth was grey and chewed off, a large portion of the cheek missing so that the teeth showed through even when the mouth was closed." The surprise in this story is the identity of the owner of the bait dogs. Like all well-wrought surprises it is prepared for and yet springs unexpected at the reader's throat.

The stories in *Father Brother Keeper* touch not only the unfamiliar but the familiar—old age, illness, family cruelty, superstition, misunderstanding repeated. "Silas" breaks an expected rhythm. Generations of farmers are beset by loss and tragedy, each father trying to make his son in his own image, until the great grandson of the first discovers in himself a talent not for farming but for carving birds. Fearful of his father's rage he buries the beautiful results of his work. But his father surprises him and us. He finds the birds and without comment builds a workshed so that his son can openly exercise his art. At the end of the story the carved birds are lined across shelves in the shed as if ready for flight, as if ready to delight us all.

—Edith Pearlman
April 14, 2013

Father Brother Keeper

A Map of the Watershed

THE SPELLS CAME LATE THAT SUMMER and left him astounded, muttering. He had known this was coming, had felt the tremors in his mind and seen familiar objects—his can of shoe polish and his TV remote—transformed in his hand into strange artifacts. The TV remote he found in his desk, facedown beside the calculator. The shoe polish was sitting in the refrigerator door beside the steak sauce.

His mind was being called back. He knew this and knew also that he wasn't ready. How impossibly fragile these old paths were, the inroads that contained his entire self, how easily choked and overgrown. That same summer he began to find himself standing in the dim backyard in early morning, his socks heavy with dew, having no idea what had brought him there, not remembering waking or half-dressing, left with the sensation that he had come out to listen, to wait for something.

———

On the wall above his desk was a map of the watershed of eastern Georgia. There were no roads or county lines, only rivers and streams and their tributaries. They lay across the surface in an arrangement that seemed as natural as the fissures in a pane of broken glass, a net of history roving above the unseen water table, the vast hornblende deposits.

His father worked for the US Geological Survey during the depression under Roosevelt, and Jim had grown up around these maps and had kept this one and had it framed. At one point in his life he could have taken a pen and paper and reproduced it in its entirety, but now he could not. Even the lakes—Weiss, Sinclair, Jackson—were becoming difficult for him, and their shapes were arbitrary. He would lie in bed and rehearse them. Some nights he could recall many. Other nights he would stir and see it there on the wall and instead of the Ogeechee and Canoochee he saw two finger-like roots that ran down from a burr in a painting so abstract it dazzled him.

The first bad episode came on his way to the bank in Waynesboro. The streets out past the hood of his truck took on a sudden shimmer before becoming slack and unfamiliar. His skin flushed—a wave of nausea, a shift in setting—as though the backdrop of a crude diorama had been pulled into place behind him. He turned, and then he took several more turns, like a draft animal, hoping his instincts might return him home.

The engine idled low, the truck running poorly. He sat through several changes of the traffic light. The muzzled exhaust amplified in his ears and Jim gripped the wheel and felt the vibrations run between his clenched knuckles. Soon other cars were backed up behind him. A man got out of a battered Buick and walked up to the driver's side window.

"Hey, you all right?" the man asked, but Jim did not answer. He looked forward in disbelief. The man reached into the cab to touch him softly on the arm, and Jim responded by laying hard on the gas. He drove through the red light. An oncoming car left long skid marks as it yelped to a stop, another went veering off into the median. Jim kept driving, kept taking turns here and there without purpose other than to keep moving. Soon the curves of the road softened and there were no shops or traffic lights, just fields full of soy in neat rows on either side and then he was tunneling through heavy pines grown tight against the long straight road.

Somewhere out past Perkins he pulled the truck into Blythe's new-and-used tire shop and took a seat on a couch in the musky waiting room, his hands folded over his lap, breathing heavily, staring at the coffee table in front of him. The table was slopped with tattered hunting magazines. The eye of a dead trophy buck glared at him from the glossed page and he didn't understand it.

The comings and goings of men, the sounds of the cash register, the caustic smells of burnt grease and cigarette smoke— all seemed a part of each other, kin in their unfamiliarity. But he knew this place, he realized. A story woke in his mind like a strange spar of knowledge. The story involved a younger man and a truck he could never get to run right. A mechanic spoke to him, wringing his hands in a soiled rag.

"How can I help you?" the mechanic asked.

"You got my timing fixed yet?" Jim asked.

"Did you drop something off?"

Jim gave his breast pockets a pat, wondered where his cigarettes were. He usually had some when he brought the truck in.

"What's the name?" the mechanic asked, lifting a clipboard from the manager's desk.

"That's my '58 Chevy you been working on," Jim said, pointing with his thumb to the garage bay over his shoulder. He crossed his legs and folded his hands in his lap, and the mechanic turned and looked at the '92 Ford parked askew underneath the front awning, the beat-up back bumper, the silver-dollar of oil forming beneath.

Jim wondered where Scott was. He and Scott Blythe would smoke together and drink coffee and talk about cars and how they weren't as good as they used to be. Soon Scott would show up and set this young fella straight.

"Where's Scott gotten off to?" Jim asked.

"Scott," the mechanic said. "You know, he's out today."

"Out?" Jim asked.

"Yeah," the mechanic said, "but we'll have you fixed up here in a minute."

"Well I ain't trying to sit here all afternoon," Jim said, still patting his shirt pockets.

"Almost done, almost done," the mechanic crooned. He picked up the phone in the back office. Eased the door shut.

A police cruiser arrived. The blue lights stunning and indistinct from the surfaces they contacted. For Jim everything dazzled. The windows. The underside of the awning. The slick of oil on the asphalt. All were of the same bright blue burning.

"You can't turn those damn things off?" the mechanic barked at the cop, guiding Jim out by the arm. Jim was shaking some now, more fragile than before, as if the story he held were thin ice spread out to the horizon, as if he knew at any moment he might spill through the feebleness of it, fall seven worlds deep through the dark, and yet where else would he go? To what other story? There is only one story and one mind. And so he waited to see what would happen and he trembled some and the young police officer leaned in through his car window and off went the lights.

When Jim came to he was sitting in the back of a police cruiser on the north side of Perkins, twenty-five miles from his home in Shell Bluff. The officer was holding his billfold—Jim could not recall having given it to him—and looking at his driver's license, asking him questions. He had lived in this part of Georgia his entire life, had been servicing his trucks at this outfit for thirty years, and he could not understand how this could have happened. The mechanic followed them home in Jim's Ford and got in with the police officer for a ride back. He told Jim to take care, told him they would get the Chevy fixed soon.

"Yeah," Jim said, "you too."

Now the decades had become a problem. Now time could wobble and reverse like a rattle-back toy. He was getting worse. After that day he decreased his orbit, quit driving altogether save for a few small trips to stores along the same road as his house, anywhere that didn't require turns.

A month later, in the middle of July, his kitchen phone rang. It was his daughter. They had not spoken since Christmas. Outside the evening dimmed and the cicadas rose into a bright wild hum. Several catocala moths gathered softly against the screen of the kitchen window and gave the square frame an abstract energy, a new unknownness.

His daughter had been living in Augusta with her new husband Ryan, a man Jim had met last December when the couple came down for the day with Callie's three-year-old twin girls.

Jim and his daughter had fallen out the year she had the twins, and Jim didn't know them except in pictures. He continually studied a Christmas card he kept in his desk, hoping to distinguish them when the time came. In the card the girls are sitting in identical reindeer pajamas and leaning precariously on each other, their names scripted beneath: Maggie and Annie. If he examined the photo long enough he thought one looked more familiar than the other, but he couldn't be certain.

The year Callie got pregnant was the year his wife Hannah was diagnosed with stage-four breast cancer—it had been there without symptoms, and had metastasized into the breast bone, lymph nodes, beneath the arms, starting into the lungs. How long had it been there, unchecked, colonizing like something under a log? Within three months of the diagnosis she was gone. For all that Jim had trouble remembering, he couldn't forget packing up his wife's curler set and bringing it to the hospital so that she could keep her hair the way she liked it. While the terminal morphine made her mind sputter and slope, the luxuriant feeling of curling her hair, the rhythm of that action, had been important to her still.

Callie and Jim had traded time in the hospital, giving each other breaks, but he thought she could have come to visit her mother more and he added that to his list of her offenses— getting pregnant and dropping out after he had paid for three years of college was at the very top; moving an hour away from

home while her mother was sick was a close second—though
he was not aware that it was his own presence, his own coldness
that had made it so difficult for her, that had made her want to
move away, to lurch at the excuse to get out of Waynesboro with
a boy. Even in those long months following the funeral they
couldn't find their way to one another. The barrier between
them seemed minor, as if it should be easily overstepped, but
it could not. It had become intrinsic, like the strange flux of
magnets turned pole to pole.

Two years later, around Christmas, he invited her to come
for a visit. They hadn't seen each other since the days immediately following the funeral. They were both changed; time
had been a friend to their grief, had pulled them through the
eye of that long year and the next, and had changed everything: Callie was recently remarried. The twins were no longer
babies. And Jim was getting scared, his age showing more now
than ever. He had mislaid a discursive piece of himself and
needed someone around who knew him. He needed light and
narration, someone who could remember, who could tell him
who he was and who knew his wife.

He called his daughter early one morning knowing she
wouldn't be awake. The phone rang for a long time and a
man's voice spoke on the answering machine and Jim left a
long erratic message with tangents he never reconciled until he
eventually ended by saying that he was sorry, though whether
he was apologizing for the message itself or something more,
something greater, even he was not sure.

When they showed up it was difficult. Jim had gotten the
house ready. He had prepared the food too early and his
daughter arrived an hour late and in between he lost focus,
grew tired. His mind loosened and he withdrew into himself

and the smile he had been planning withered. By the time they arrived he was slightly cold, distant.

Ryan's clothing was loose-fitting. The baggy white shirt drooped from his neck, exposing a gold chain that lay in the hair of his chest. The oversized jean shorts fell over his knee-caps and his thick legs seemed spindled, without joints. Jim had never seen a man like him. He had a large tattoo on his right calf of an old patriarchal cross with script beneath that said "Rest in Peace Bobby."

His daughter put the twins down on the floor of the living room where Jim could watch them. Callie wandered slowly through the house, picking up certain objects and holding them for long periods before putting them back down again: framed pictures, his wife's bird book, a small antique sad-iron. I have kept her from her home, Jim thought, as he watched her tour the unchanging house.

The girls played with the set of his wife's old curlers while Jim rocked nervously in his Barcalounger. There were long pauses in the conversation while the two men sat staring at the twins as if they were a campfire and it was late and nothing needed to be said.

Callie eventually disappeared into the back bedroom and the scene played out in Jim's mind. She would go into her mother's closet, pull the string on the light, and stand there amongst the clothing, the shoes, the heavy smell of her mother's perfume. She would examine the vials and powders sitting in place on the bathroom counter. She would try to form a voice, a presence of some kind, out of these things. The presence would escape her, fall short of memory, and she would imagine that this was her fault somehow.

Jim looked at the open doorway that led from the kitchen

to the back bedroom and he longed to get up and check on Callie, to ask her how she was, but he couldn't move. One of the twins held up a penny she found in the carpet and pursued a timid path over to him to deliver it.

"Thank you," he said to the girl.

"What do we say?" Ryan barked, startling both the girl and Jim.

The girl looked around for her mother, confused.

"What do we say? Say, You're welcome, Mr. Jim. You're welcome."

The girl looked at Ryan and pushed her hair out of her face and sat back down again on the carpet with her sister and said nothing. Ryan looked at Jim and shrugged and Jim looked down at the girls again, embarrassed. His daughter finally came back from the bedroom with a few pieces of jewelry—a locket and some rings, she said—and asked if she could keep them. Jim nodded and didn't look at the hand she held out, didn't want to.

Ryan had a case of beer and he drank five of them before they sat down to dinner. He went outside to smoke often, talking on his phone to friends, laughing so loud you could hear his breath whistle. "I heard that," he heaved over and over again into the cell phone. He treaded small pieces of gravel from the walkway outside into the house, caught in the soles of his boots, so that Jim found the little pebbles for weeks, hidden in the cheap Berber. The young man talked more as he drank and every time he spoke it seemed his voice grew louder and higher until it rang against the walls of the kitchen.

Jim felt a tremendous relief once their car finally pulled away. Though he was ashamed of himself, ashamed to be glad to be rid of his daughter's company, he was more relieved than anything else. He dreaded having to be around that man again. He could feel the emptiness of his house behind him as he waved goodbye to the girls in the back seat. For a long time he stood in the dark side yard looking off into the woods. In the hot creatured buzz of the early evening he closed his eyes and considered praying but he could not manage it.

His wife's prayers had been simple statements—he could rehearse them at length but they remained permanently her own—underpinned with a sense of reaching, a desire to understand herself, to know the impossible. Jim had found the hidden nature of religion to be like a doorway sealed off a long time ago. If there is a god, he thought, his followers must be running on fumes by now.

The temptation to pray was not new but had come when the spells came. But it seemed strange or sentimental to take on so simply a habit that had always been hers. He sat at his kitchen table and smoked cigarettes and drank cold coffee until the desire faded; then he slept some, though poorly. He dreamed intermittently and it was a dream with no real facts, just fragments, scraps of nothing. Everything was abstract but imbued with great restlessness and urgency so that he would wake from the dream only to fall soundly back into it. His father's rivers were no longer mounted on the wall over the desk but instead on the ceiling over his bed. They seemed to squirm and roll like a knot of vipers. He woke in sheets slick with sweat.

When his daughter called, Jim was cleaning a boiled chicken. The phone had not rung in many weeks and it jarred him. He had forgotten it was there. The knife slipped and his weight went forward with it, moving across the top of the pointer finger on his left hand.

"It's your nickel," he said into the receiver, holding up the hand as the blood decanted into the cleft between his fingers. He wrapped up the finger in a paper towel without seeing where it was cut exactly. His daughter's voice came through the receiver, tiny and remote. "I need to ask you for a favor."

"Hey, sugar."

Two red splotches bloomed across the surface of the towel. Etowah Lake, he thought. He was feeling good. He threw the towel away and grabbed another.

"Can I use your truck for a few hours tomorrow morning?"

"I haven't been driving it much lately. I'll see if it's got gas. What happened to your car?"

"Ryan sold it. Would you mind watching the girls for the morning? I've got to run some errands."

He responded with a long silence. Jim squared his shoes with the checkered pattern in the linoleum floor. He needed to answer but had never imagined being alone with the girls.

When the doctor told Jim and Hannah they were pregnant it seemed an impossibility, an echo come back twenty years too late. He would turn fifty-three that year; Hannah would turn forty-five. They had made the appointment because Hannah was having bad headaches and back pain, expecting this least of all things. They asked if there had been a mistake with the blood work. They asked to check the spelling of their last name. They asked if they could listen, if they could hear a heartbeat. Soon there were no questions left and they sat together in the examination room staring, relearning the old mixed feelings, all the years they had tried to get pregnant with no luck, the hope that ran parallel against their suspicion that it would never happen. And yet they had done it. And didn't that prove that they were capable of anything, that all things were possible?

"What's your husband got going?" Jim asked.

"Working."

He thought suddenly about telling her. How could he say it? He thought he should say something about the spells, getting lost in the car, and then immediately he thought of losing his house, being put up somewhere, and he thought better of it all. He could do it. He could make it work.

"So when you coming by?"

He got out of bed at five that next morning, took a shower, shaved his face carefully and dressed himself in the clothing he had laid out across his desk chair the night before: a pair of khaki pants and a silky red collared shirt, a golden eagle embroidered on the breast pocket where he put his cigarettes, two pencils, reading glasses, and a yellow Bic lighter.

He made coffee and sat down at the table with his heart pounding. He laid one palm flat on the table top and lifted it slowly to watch the waning of the foggy shadow it left behind. It was late summer but the early morning left the kitchen dim and chilly. He took a few sips of coffee and watched the dark pull up from out back of his house like a curtain being lifted deep behind the trees. A light growing at the edge of the world, a soft blue that rose higher as morning came. The kitchen warmed and he felt more like himself. His mind cleared and his hands steadied and he felt good.

A little after nine he heard Ryan's car pull up into the gravel. Callie was standing outside the passenger door and they were exchanging harsh words. Her face was taut, her eyes sunken. She helped the girls out from behind the seats and snapped at him before slamming the door. Jim stepped back from the window and waited for the bell to ring.

When he opened the door his daughter was standing there looking loose and exhausted, the girls' hands in hers. Ryan was gone. The smell of exhaust hung in the air.

Callie said the girls hadn't eaten anything and that she was in a hurry. Jim never ate breakfast at home anymore, just coffee. He should have thought of that, should have thought to pick up food.

"We'll get breakfast at Lake's," he said. "Drop us off and we'll get us some breakfast and wait on you." He made his way into the passenger seat of his own truck and sat down before his daughter could hand him the keys. The girls piled in between them.

As they walked into the restaurant he turned to wave to his daughter. Callie's smile struck him as strange, rigid. Something was off but he could not place it. He picked up one of the girls and watched as his daughter drove away. He led the other girl slowly by the hand and the waitress saw them and got the door open. She knelt down to meet the girl at Jim's side after saying hello. Jim felt very proud suddenly.

"My Lord, what do you have here? Oh my Lord."

"You haven't met my grandbabies?" Jim said.

"Are they twins? Oh my Lord," said the woman.

"This one here was out a minute before this other." He lowered his head and shook the hand of the other little girl who was leaning into the leg of his pants. "I think they're still half asleep," he said, as an apology.

"How old are they?"

"They'll be three in December. I think they're on the smaller end of things and so they look younger than they are. I used to get 'em mixed up but now they're about as different as can be. This one here is quiet as a mouse. Say, ain't I? Ain't I?"

He shook the girl by the hand again.

"You still have them boost-up seats?"

"Yeah. I'll bring 'em out."

The woman disappeared around the corner to the kitchen and the old man entered into the familiar dining room, leading the girls into the back corner where his booth was over against the window. He realized suddenly that the booster seats wouldn't fit against the table there and turned back, scanned the restaurant. He sat down at a freestanding table farther away from the window than he normally liked.

The girls ate their breakfast quickly. They were hungry. They gripped the utensils with small fists and their eating was clumsy. Yet some of their gestures—the brushing of hair from their faces, the turn of a head to look out the window—were so familiar, so feminine, so much like his wife's.

Annie, the smaller, the one that most looked like family, had a birthmark on her neck just below her ear. He put his hand lightly on the spot and covered it with his thumb. He petted their heads. It all felt good to him, sitting there with his granddaughters, and he found himself less anxious and he wondered what his wife would think if she could see this. He imagined her love for these girls, the power of it. He promised himself he would see them more.

After breakfast the waitress brought coloring books and a bundle of crayons wrapped up in a rubber band. Soon the crayons covered the table and a musky earthy odor mixed with the smell of his coffee. The girls colored a few pages each, sometimes getting Jim to help and at other times pushing his hand away. Soon Annie grew restless and wanted to get down. Jim helped her out of her chair. She wanted to go to the window. He moved them both out of their booster seats and sat them in the booth. They stood up to look out.

They looked out on the lake and watched some coots darting down beneath the surface of the water. Jim pointed to this or that but they were ready to go. He checked his watch. It was twelve. The girls' restlessness had an edge on it now and he was getting worried. The lunch crowd was appearing. A number of paper-mill workers, smelling of sulfur and sour sweat, drifted into the restaurant and occupied the tables around them.

Jim's eyes drifted out to the parking lot every time a car pulled in; they darted to the door when it chimed. The strange look on his daughter's face as she pulled away now consumed him. She hadn't said a word. The thought struck him hard. He hadn't missed anything. She had simply gotten out, put her daughters on the sidewalk beside him, and driven off. Something was wrong with that. Something was wrong with the way she left them.

He bought the girls ice cream and tried some soup and a few crackers but his hands were shaking and he couldn't eat it. The sounds of the restaurant around him amplified: the men from the mill laughing, the clatter of tableware, the orders being called out behind him. The restaurant lost its warmth and homeliness. He couldn't do anything but keep waiting, though something in him knew now that she wasn't going to show.

At the end of that hour both girls started to cry and he could not quiet or calm them. It was three in the afternoon. They had both wet themselves through their pull-ups and Jim realized that he hadn't taken them to the bathroom. He asked the wait-ress to sit with the girls while he used the phone in the kitchen. He called his house twice in case she was there. Both times the phone rang until he heard his own recorded voice, more frail than he thought he sounded, "This is Jim. Leave a message."

He pored through the phonebook trying to find his daugh-ter's number in Augusta but as he got to the B's he couldn't remember Ryan's last name, the girls' last names, his daugh-ter's new last name—nothing would come and then he wasn't certain if it started with a B at all. He returned to his table where the girls were howling. The street outside wavered, the heat twisting the air over the asphalt.

The restaurant manager was at their table now and the waitress was explaining the situation.

"This morning," she said. "I don't know, a little after nine."

"Jesus," the manager said, licking his lips as his gears ran.

Maggie stuck out her arms, reaching up for Jim. He picked her up and held Annie by the hand and the manager escorted the three of them into a small office behind the kitchen. They passed through a small corridor beside the stove behind the cook. In the crowded back office the two girls wept more like two young women, silently, out of exhaustion.

The manager asked Jim who he should call to get them and he had no answer. He had no other family. Almost without deciding to he tried to tell the man what he couldn't even tell his daughter, what he hadn't told anyone.

"I've been having some spells," he said. "I lose track every now and then, and then I don't know. I don't drive much."

"Do you know where you are?" the manager asked, sud-denly shouting as though there were a wall between them. Jim nodded.

The man got on the phone and within a few minutes a young police officer arrived and walked them out through the kitchen's back door.

The spell didn't start until they got in the officer's car. Jim couldn't remember where he lived. That one bit of missing information was like the focal point in a piece of burning film. He tried to picture his home but the image wouldn't come. The unfamiliar was spreading out. He hadn't brought his wallet, only a fold of cash. The officer looked at him as the questions stalled painfully.

"Sir, do you live here in Waynesboro?"

Ryan came into the county office and grabbed the girls by their arms and pulled them up out of their seats.

"Girls, come on," he said, taking them by their hands.

Jim had come to recognize the girls but little else. Hearing Ryan's voice was a kind of recognition, though it wasn't complete. He mistook him for a boy who used to live down the street, sold insurance. He couldn't understand what the boy wanted with the girls. Jim rose out of his seat and tried to hold the girls back.

"You with her on this thing? She staying with you now? She's nearly killed herself. Do you know that?"

Ryan moved his face up close to Jim's. Jim didn't know what the boy meant to do. When Ryan tried again to take the girls Jim held them back and Ryan shoved the old man against the seats behind him. An officer stepped in, told Ryan to go or he'd arrest him. Jim watched from the ground as Ryan lifted up the girls, watched them gripping his shoulders. He laid his head on the floor in total confusion, felt his eyes fill with hot tears, a bitter pain in his throat. He was losing traction.

———

A paint crew off Twin Ponds Road in Sparta found his truck lying on its side. The men had quit work and were driving out to park and to drink their tallboys at the end of the day when the light was easy and the evening cool. Two ink-black skid marks converged and twisted where she cranked the wheel, ending in the high grass at the low shoulder where the truck rolled down. They saw her through the front glass lying face up on the downward window, unconscious, her legs over the steering wheel as if she had propped them there, the radio tuned to an old gospel station broadcasting from somewhere in Wrens. Out past the skid marks, lying with all its hooves on the white line—was a dead doe, the fur almost gray, several ribs deviating strangely from their natural arcs.

The bed of the truck was half-full of her possessions, the other half scattered all over the shoulder of the road and some down into the hardwoods, clothing in piles, shoes, some books and magazines, framed pictures of her with the girls, her with her first boyfriend; she had cleared everything out of the house, left no memory of herself there. And where was she going?

The truck had stalled but the engine was still hot. The men broke the front window by her feet and the smell of gas and monoxide rose heavily. They opened the door and dragged her out and laid her on a paint tarp and waited there for the ambulance. Her face was pale, the nose elegant, the skin smooth like bone. There was a tiny speck of lint stuck to her lip and one of the men pulled it off carefully, as if he were worried about waking her.

They watched her labored breathing and fanned her face with an empty paint tray. They stared at her dresses piled in the back of the truck. They imagined the floral prints against her skin, the sound of her voice. Blood pooled slowly inside her ear, an aquifer recharging, blooming up to the earth, and when they saw it they turned her over so that it ran over her lips and onto the tarp beneath her. In the distance the sound of a siren grew and one of the men, stationed at the turn in the road, waved at it madly until it turned.

When the officer dropped Jim off, Callie was unconscious, still critical. He had come back around to find his daughter near the edge of something deep. Head trauma and hypoxia, the doctor said. Jim remembered the familiar sounds of the place, the young nurses, always rubbing hand sanitizer on as they came in and out of the room, examining their gear. It did not seem long enough to be back here. After a few moments the attending ER doctor came and shook his hand.

"I told Ryan earlier," he said, "she came this close." He held up his thumb and forefinger as if to pinch the space, the tiny helpless seed that is death in each of us, set between his fingers. "That cab was full of exhaust. It's a miracle she's still alive."

Ryan did not return that evening. Jim stayed in her hospital room for several hours, watching the heart rate and blood pressure go through their small permutations on the monitor above her bed. She wore an oxygen mask and an oxygen monitor attached to her finger tip. Nurses recorded its slow constant rise on a chart. She was climbing back from the depth she had achieved as the oxygen bound again to the blood.

In the night a nurse woke him. She knew his name and asked if she could drive him home. He slept the entire ride, the nurse following him inside his house, laying him in his bed with his shoes on. He felt so weak, a kind of exhaustion he had never known in his life, as if he himself had been in that wreck, and come back from the edge. He felt the nurse untying his shoes, putting them gently on the floor. He knew he recognized her and that she must have known his wife, but he could not bear to ask. He imagined that she was one of the twins, fully grown, loving, strong. "Annie?" he asked.

He woke desperate to see his daughter, a necessity like thirst. The wrecker called the house early and Jim requested the truck be towed to a used-car lot owned by the son of an old friend. He didn't want to see it.

"Whatever you get for it," he said, "just let me know and we'll talk."

"What about her stuff?" the man asked.

Her possessions from the truck bed, and whatever could be found in the grass and woods, were all wrapped up in a giant paint tarp like a bindle. Jim didn't have their address and didn't know what Callie would want to do anyway, and so the wrecker left the pile sitting in Jim's carport.

He walked out to the carport and threw back the folds of the tarp. He held up a framed picture of his daughter and Ryan at the state fair—both their faces splotched, slightly drunk; his daughter's smile showing strain, a subtle imperceptible withdrawal from the man beside her. He put down the frame and began to drag her clothing inside, most of it still attached to the hangers. He piled it onto the sofa.

He called the hospital several times and was told his daughter was still not conscious. He sat by the kitchen table against the window and looked out across the empty yard, the grass overgrown, tufts of clover appearing, bands of light crashing through the limbs of the sycamore, strewn shadows of various shade thrusting over the grass with the wind. He saw images of the twins. He saw Annie's birthmark and he winced remembering the horrible things he had said and, even worse, thought about his daughter when she got pregnant.

He was in the backyard standing in front of a curtain of wisteria blooming down a white ash tree. The phone sounded like a bird calling. The phone, he told himself. He ran into the house and caught it on its last ring.

"Hello?"

"Jim?"

"Yeah."

He guessed it was Ryan.

"She's up now. Won't talk to me. Said she wants to see you."

In the breeze the faded pink birdfeeder adjusted itself against the kitchen window.

"You need a ride?" Ryan asked

"Where are the girls?" Jim asked.

"My mom's got 'em. So you need a ride?"

"Yeah," Jim said. "Thank you."

They rode out past the row-crop fields toward the hospital, the cooling tower from the nuclear plant looming high above the road, huge billows of white steam rolling up into the sky, crumpled over the horizon like cotton. Cloud factory, he used to tell his daughter when they drove along this road. The furrows raced along beside the car, pushed along like a wave, like the comb of a feather.

"You didn't seem to recognize me the other day," Ryan said.

"I had forgotten who you were."

Ryan didn't know how to take that. "Well, anyway," he continued, "I'm sorry about all that. I didn't mean to get so angry. I was confused, and you were confused," he said.

"Okay," Jim said.

They pulled into a gas station across the street from the hospital. Ryan let the truck idle for a minute. He seemed nervous. Jim put his hand on the door handle.

"You know I would never hurt them girls," Ryan said. "They ain't mine, but I would never hurt them. Callie has some notion about me, but she gets confused and doesn't know what she's saying."

Jim looked at the man his daughter had married. He looked young and exhausted, at the limits. Callie had found a bruise on one of those girls, Jim thought suddenly. Something. To leave the way she did, to throw everything she owned into that truck, Jim knew something had happened and he regretted now letting Ryan give him a ride.

"Will you tell her?" he asked.

"Tell her?"

"Tell her that you and I had an argument?"

"No," Jim said, getting out of the truck. "I won't." And that was true. He didn't need to. Callie had made up her mind. He knew that much.

———

The place was brighter in the daylight, the sterile hallways packed full of gear and trays. Jim realized he had not showered in some time. He hadn't even looked at himself in a mirror. He diverted into the bathroom. He stood before the mirror. His thin hair was greasy. Tufts were sticking out. He ran some water into his palm and matted it down, splashed water on his face and held his cool hands against his eyes. They were swollen. Nothing would help that. He tucked in his shirt and then untucked it, and then tucked it in again.

They had moved her to a new room directly across from the nurse's station. Her name had been written on a white board outside the door: Callie Williamson. She was lying very still, an IV in the top of the hand that rested across her stomach, one of the plastic capsules near the skin full of bright red blood. He walked in the door but not much farther, standing clear as a tech moved around the bed. Her eyes were bruised, hooded, and discolored. The right was full of blood and seemed to drift. When the tech turned, Jim's hand flinched once at his side, as if it might rise and offer itself.

He was a large black man with powerful shoulders and long hair in tight braids. Jim had never felt comfortable around such men. He gave him lots of room. The tech pulled out a chair and placed it beside the large bed and motioned for Jim to have a seat. Jim looked out the window and then he looked at his hands and rubbed them as if they were cold.

"It's all right, Dad," Callie said.

Jim sat down in the chair and watched as the tech left the room.

"I have your clothes," he eventually thought to say. "I brought 'em in the house. Some is real muddy but not all. You can come stay there if you like, since your stuff is there. You and the girls, if you like."

She nodded and smiled.

"I saw something standing in the road," she said after some time.

"It was a doe," he said.

"Yeah, they told me it was. I thought maybe it was a little boy."

Jim shook his head no. He leaned forward and thought he would touch her but he did not. She closed her eyes and seemed to be falling asleep.

"I'm leaving Ryan," she said.

"I thought so."

"I know Mom would hate it."

"No," he said, "she wouldn't hate anything."

She turned her hand over and held it out. In her palm were the rivers he had named so many years ago, teaching her each name, tracing them with his pointer finger—the Tugaloo, Black Creek, Sapelo. They converged below her thumb into the Savannah Basin. He lowered his face into her palm and they rushed into his mind, culminating like a long-coming prayer that forms high in the Seed Lake watershed of early spring, bright and clean and harmless, and comes barreling down after the summer storms with irresistible power, now heavy and now full of salt in the low country.

Fallow Dog

Every year strangers drive along the power-line easement and dump trash on the back of his grandfather's land. He has never seen them but he finds their bald tire prints in the clay, their empty energy drinks shining in the dallisgrass. He imagines they are nervous people, people in a rush. They see the spot from the road and pull off.

Soon a small landfill forms where the power lines cut south and at the end of each year his grandfather pays someone with a front-end loader to haul it off, a fresh start.

All his life it seemed strange to him what could be learned about the lives of others from what they left behind—whether they were in a rush, had young children, whether they changed their own tires and oil, whether they used a fake Christmas tree. He could assemble their lives in his mind this way; not accurately, but meaningfully, in detail.

It was the day after his grandfather's funeral. He had told his father he would drive down to the property and pick up a few things, repost the scattered trespass signs on the back of the land, check the gates. He expected to find the usual—a discarded washer and dryer set full of dirt dauber nests; milk jugs heavy with used transmission oil the misgiving color of blood; a waterlogged mattress; used car batteries; a faded toy kitchen covered with crayon markings—the kind of stuff people get rid of when their homes foreclose and they have to clear out quick and don't want to risk having their out-of-date tags run by a cop at the county dump.

What he found that morning was a number of upended industrial barrels shining blue against the autumn field. Fifty-gallon chemical drums, spaced out evenly, in a line facing away from the road. From inside them came a sound like a record-ing being played, throated and hollow, the whimper and bay of anxious dogs. He stared at the drums for some time and tried to make sense of it but could not. Someone dumped a litter of puppies here, but *inside the drums?*

A light rain began. Everything to the east was soaked in light and the light was strewn over the trees across the ease-ment as if it were shining bleakly through a scrim. The effect was not what he remembered. He remembered the strong green of soy and the beautiful crawl of the center pivot drap-ing mist on a bright day, the light clinging easy to the wet air over the field like diaphanous flame, like gossamer, those days when his grandfather Septimus was still alive and his great-un-cle Oct was planting three seasons out of the year in the adjoin-ing fields, all row crops, all beautiful and neat. Jimmy had not been back here to visit in several years, since moving away after college, and the place had changed almost beyond recogni-tion, the fields now gray and disheveled and full of common invasive plants, the pivot rusty and motionless. These last cou-ple of years Septimus had been too sick to take care of things and as far as Jim knew, in all that time, no one had walked the back of the property. It did not surprise him to find something had gone wrong.

The barrels were open on one end and faced away from him. He'd never seen the like but he knew. Someone had built make-shift kennels here and the dogs were being baited to fight.

Inside the trailer it was very cold, shaded heavily by old live oaks. Earlier that morning the chain across the entrance road lay an inch deep in mud. He had drug it out and laid it in a wet coil slop at the base of the post. He washed the mud off his hands in the kitchen sink and found his grandfather's cereal bowl and spoon sitting right there, as if the old man had just finished his breakfast and would be standing behind him, standing with his coffee by the window.

He was tempted to set a fire in the chimney insert and to sit down in Sept's old Barcalounger, pull the heavy quilts over his clothing and just let sleep come, to listen to the whine and pop of well-cured hardwood and drift off, imagining that none of it had ever happened, that there had been no funeral and that the town was not emptying itself of good people like a broken silo. But he didn't want to wake up there with the fire out and the room cold again, realizing anew that Sept was gone. The knowledge that he did not want to be here told him he was growing older and growing away from this place.

Here he'd learned to drive one summer afternoon with Oct in his big battered Dodge Ram, the large steering wheel loose in his hands as they moved over the soft dirt at the field's edge. Those days gave him the sensation that the world was a pliable, forgiving place. His great-uncle let Jimmy circle the field as long as he wanted, Oct sitting back with his arm across the seat rest behind his head, singing low beneath the turned-up radio.

When his grandmother passed away his grandfather mourned by selling their house in Augusta, the home they had built away from the rural world of his family, a place they had made with the money he earned selling insurance. The trailer in Shell Bluff had been his hunting cabin but he made it his permanent home now, a place to retire and be near his brother.

He was finally away from the city again, away from the constant hum of advertisements, the new car dealerships that colonized the freeways and simmered through the night until the stars were washed out. He had put it all behind him in the last years of his life. It was a kind of repentance. He would live beside his brother again and watch his brother work and help when he could.

Behind a row of shoes still wet with Kiwi shine, he found the .22 beneath the bed. It smelled to Jimmy like childhood, like 3-In-One oil. He pulled the gun out and opened the bedside drawer and stirred the socks and underwear for the box of .22 longs. He poured the entire contents of the box into his coat pocket and headed for the front door.

It was cold for Georgia in early November. The light rain made his clothing damp and the chill was getting through. It put a cinch high up around his chest and made his breathing shallow. As he looked out at the barrels he regretted not bringing the heavy Winchester. The trailer was forty acres behind him. The woods that sloped down from the trailer to this back field were thick with undergrowth and fallen trees; the fire breaks overgrown and barricaded with large knotted limbs, rotten and broken in the heavy storms of summer. The walking would take too much time. He would not go back for it.

He began to count the barrels laid out in front of him as they came into sight. In the distance, across the abandoned field, the galvanized trusses of the old center pivot loped in and out of the grass and pine saplings. The distant woods across, toward the neighbor's property, lay heavy and darkening in his mind. Jimmy tried again to remember the last time he heard anything from Sept about who bought the land out past the power line easement but the name wouldn't come. It was at least five years ago that Oct sold that portion.

He could hear the dogs stirring now. The breeze had changed and they could smell him. He put his hand into his right pocket and felt the slender .22 casings. He loaded a few into the breech and flipped the safety and tucked the stock into his shoulder.

He came up slow and stepped around the front of the first drum in a wide arc, widening the angle between the sight and the dark opening. This one was empty. He let out a breath, lowering the muzzle to the ground. The open side of the drum faced a heavy ceramic chimney cover, a makeshift bowl full of cloudy water. Beside the barrel was a large carriage bolt driven into the earth, two inches thick, its head bright and hard, worn from hammer strikes. From the stake ran what looked to be three feet of rusted chain attached to a galvanized pipe shackle, a collar. Holding the shackle in his hand sent a chill through his body.

The neighbor that bought the adjacent land must have thought himself real clever to put his kennels just over the property line. He wished then his father would have come down here with him. He took his time now, feeling himself thrust into an adult world, feeling a familial responsibility. He thought about the thickness of the chains and wondered how deep the carriage bolts sat, if they ran down into the clay or just through the top soil and if a dog that size could work it loose. He bet it could. Some of the stakes might already have fallen over with the heavy rains. A few of the dogs were barking now.

He made his way slowly into the line of barrels, expecting a bull terrier or a big Spanish bull to be lying there in the grass. What he found seemed to be the size of a pony: a bull mastiff, the fur down its back and sides brindled like a tiger. The immense cage of ribs lay on its side, throbbing slowly. It must have weighed 150 pounds. He held his breath for a moment and watched the dog stand as he drew closer and as it stood it seemed to grow in size again. He put the sights on it and let his finger rest on the safety and came forward a little more.

He was surprised when the dog did not bare its teeth. Forward more and still it showed no aggression. It did not fight against the end of its chain or square off. It only stood and even that seemed out of politeness, a greeting. The ears had been docked down so low they showed like craters against its head; the tail was docked entirely; there was almost no way to read its mood. Jimmy kept walking still, cooing softly. All the dogs were standing now, some barking. "Hey bud. Hey buddy," Jim said. The big eyes moved away from his, as if it were embarrassed by something, while the nostrils dilated, taking him in. The right side of the dog's mouth showed itself gray and chewed off, a large portion of the cheek missing so that the teeth showed through even when the mouth was closed. The left eye was full of blood and the other the lifeless gray of slate. There were cotton wads packed into a deep gash across the top of its head.

Jimmy neared it and the animal remained right where it was. He put out his hand and the dog came forward to sniff it and seemed disappointed, anxious. Jimmy sat down on the edge of the barrel and carefully ran his hand down the animal's neck and brought the hand back covered in dark oxidized blood. Its size was terrific and it was strangely comforting sitting there with him now, listening to the rain alight softly in the field. He imagined the size of the dog's heart, he imagined the heart growing in a series of glass jars all its life, each labeled week to week, until the heart, at twenty-five weeks, overflowed the jars.

This was a veteran, he thought, a winner—and this the laurel: this field, this day. And now no one would bet against him, which would explain why there was no food or water in his bowl, why he'd been left out here to die. Jimmy took the mastiff's bowl and walked with it up over the high bank of the irrigation pond and down the crater to where the latest rains had collected and scooped the dog some water. He brought it back slow not to spill it and set it down.

"Come here, sir," Jimmy said as he stirred his finger in the water. The dog did not move. He brought the bowl up to the torn face and it sniffed and began to lap. He set the bowl down and watched the dog empty it and then almost immediately vomit the water up.

Inside him something fell away, descending into a great sadness and darkness of spirit. It was like a blade once held against his neck in middle school. It was a small black boy who held the blade, a boy who lived with six older brothers in a trailer off the clay road behind his neighborhood, a sick grin on the face so close to his own before the bright thing was put away, the bright thing that had held his whole mind for that long moment on its small edge. A smell of kerosene heat in the boy's clothing. A badly cut lip on the boy's face, where the swelling had just started. Someone had struck the boy and the boy had left the someone and had come up on Jimmy in the woods and now this, now a knife? A joke? A peal of laughter. Alone now with his deep deep sadness and a tiny nick in his neck that stunk with his sweat and the black boy was the only boy laughing and the laughter rang like bells in the woods and then the boy was gone and it was exactly like this moment, fear and sadness and the mixture amalgamating into shame.

He found there were thirteen others. Mostly bull terriers, though there was one big pinscher, unmarked and well fed, an investment perhaps, and one shepherd, its fur heavily matted with blood like the mastiff's but with no wounds of its own. Two others were already dead and lay festering—either from infection or dehydration, he didn't know. Bait dogs with their teeth filed down to soft nubs like stones, scabs from the duct tape their owners had wrapped around their muzzles. Two more lay breathing but would not stand, their eyes rolling languidly as Jimmy lifted the lids. The eyes stirred his anger, stirred it like poison in his blood. He noticed the buzzards now, the wake sitting in perfect silence and patience along the top pin of the power lines, at least eight of them spread out across the utility poles, a procession as calculated as man. They had been down here feeding on some of these. They would start with the eyes.

The sadness wound his mind like a spring and before he had decided what to do he sighted the farthest buzzard in the breast with the rifle and eased the safety across the trigger guard and felt his anger clarify and the iron sight grow impossibly still until it covered the large bird completely. He made a slow fist around the trigger and watched the ugly bird fall off the top pin of the pole before the sound crossed the field and echoed back. He winged another buzzard as it tried to get off, a moving shot, and it fell into the far field and loped and he shot it again at a great distance.

Inside him a scale had been slowly tipping; a hard knot grew in his throat and burned there beneath his jaw. He went back to the mastiff and put the rifle barrel against the side of its temple and shot it twice, two hard snaps. The air hardened with cartridge fouling and sulfite. The dog dropped near the opening of the drum. He moved on to the others. He visited each one with the rifle. After he visited them he kicked their water bowls and removed their collars and slung their chains far into the field. He petted their damp skulls and held their large paws in his hands. When the rain came on strong he left them and sat down nearby in the cover of the trees and watched for a while. Once he thought they might still be breathing and the thought made his heart pound. He went out to them again only to realize they were not, only in his mind. Another buzzard returned and he took aim but he found himself shivering, his eyes wet.

It was well into the afternoon when he got back to the trailer, three casings left in his pocket. He took off his shirt and threw it into the trash and washed his face and arms. He had set the neighbor back at least seven grand, if not more—not counting fight winnings—over the course of just an hour and it had only cost him about four bucks in .22 rounds and his breakfast, which he threw up on the walk back.

In Sept's closet he found the old over-and-under 20 gauge. The shells were lying on the floor by a pile of shoes in a plastic bag. They were old. He checked the primers and put a few in his back pocket and stuck two into the breech of the gun, hearing the shells seal each barrel like a plug. He recognized an old shirt hanging in the closet, slightly too big for him, the front pockets worn and stretched out from Sept's glasses, tobacco, and pens. He put the shirt on. It smelled sweet like Levi Garrett with a trace of pomade.

The truck moved easy onto the rutted driveway, the shotgun lying against the passenger seat beside him. Dust, hidden beneath the light falling of rain, curled in two thick waves behind the truck as he turned down the road along the field's edge beneath the power lines, heading toward the neighbor's property, heading to get something started though he didn't know what.

He was surprised to see how big the neighbor's house was. Most people out there lived in mobile homes. This guy had a two story house with white vinyl siding and an above-ground swimming pool. No dogs were out and there were no kennels. Off to the right, alongside the driveway, an old rake implement and a set of disks were both half-sunk into the ground, centipede weeds pushing up through them. They were Oct's old implements, he recognized them, and it hurt to see them sitting out like decorations, antique collectibles, novelties.

He knocked twice and heard the sound of small footfall on

the carpeted steps inside. The door opened quickly and a little blonde girl was standing in front of him, pushing her hair out of her face with the palm of her hand. Behind her a cartoon was playing on a TV. A few magazines and some puzzle pieces were scattered over the floor.

"Your daddy home?" Jimmy asked.

"He's at work," she said, wiping her eyes. He couldn't tell how old she was, seven, eight at the most, too young to be alone here.

"What about your momma?"

"She's running barons," she said.

"Barons, huh?"

"Yeah."

"Tell your daddy that Jimmy Williamson wants..." The girl rubbed her eyes again. "Never mind," he said. He turned back to his truck as the girl went back to the sofa without shutting the front door. He looked back from the sidewalk, came back and shut the door for her.

He started the motor and sat feeling the engine's vibration in his body. He couldn't decide if he would pull down the drive a bit and wait or just call the cops and let them deal with him. If he did call they would only fine him, if that. You could only get in real trouble dog fighting in Georgia if you're caught at the scratch line and that hardly ever happened. The pits were so deep in the woods, usually on someone else's land or hidden in hunt clubs down by festering marshes, and that's assuming the cops weren't the ones fighting to begin with.

Now Jimmy worried this guy would find his dogs all shot and come back that night and wreck or burn out Sept's trailer— not that it was worth much but it was worth something. With no one there it would be an easy target, a simple gesture.

He pulled the truck around and started down the drive. At the far end of the long dirt drive a green Chevy pulled in off Shell Bluff Road and started toward the house. He rolled down his driver's-side window, pulling off the lane, and put the shot-gun across the bench with the stock facing him so that he could reach it through the window if he needed to. He stepped out and leaned against his door and waited for the man to come alongside.

The Chevy pulled up slowly, idling rough. The driver was a short middle-aged man with red cheeks and reddish blond hair that curled up by his ears beneath his work hat. He was wearing a dark blue uniform from the pulp mill. The smell of ammonium sulfite drifted out of his truck's cab and mixed with the hard sweetness of the diesel exhaust. He had a name tag on his shirt that said D. Garner and there was a rifle on a rack in the window behind his head.

"How is it?" he said to Jimmy, looking slightly pleased to have encountered someone in his driveway. He stuck out his hand. Jimmy started in quickly, ignoring the gesture.

"You own this tract now?" he said coldly, staring at the man's jawline. The man was chewing tobacco, leaning over to spit it into a cup he held between his legs.

"I do, bought it from Octavius Williamson a few years ago. You mind me asking what I can help you with?" The man's hand now rested palm down on the window cowling.

Jimmy looked down the road and wondered how to proceed.

"I'm Jimmy Williamson," he began. "Septimus Williamson is my grandfather. Oct is my uncle."

"I could have guessed that," the man said. "I haven't had the chance to meet Sept since I came down here, but I've heard awfully good things about him. I keep meaning to get by there soon and pay him a visit and introduce myself but he is rarely around. How is he getting on?"

"He passed three days ago," Jimmy said.

"Well," the man said, "I am sorry to hear that." He sat back into his seat and looked up the road toward his house in a solemn manner and then spat some Skoal out into the cup and put it back between his legs.

"I came down here to check our lines yesterday. I walked the back of the property just this morning and found something interesting. You know anything about that?" Jimmy didn't let the man answer, though he didn't look like he intended to. "I need you to get what's left of it cleaned off. I don't give a damn what you do on your own time, but I expect that kind of mess to stay off our property. And I particularly don't appreciate someone taking advantage of Sept that way, especially while he was sick." Jimmy's head seemed to swell, the air around him electric. He glanced behind him at the stock of the shotgun and then back at the man in his truck and thought again of the dogs and the great sadness and the anger. The man turned his engine off, as if it was interfering with his hearing. He leaned out the window and looked hard at Jimmy.

"I'm afraid you're going to have to spell this out for me son. I don't know you what for the thirty seconds you been standing there, but if you're going to accuse me of something you can come right out with it."

"I found a bunch of filthy scratch mutts sitting just across Sept's property line earlier this morning. Some should have been put down they were so mistreated. I know they didn't belong to nobody I know."

"Didn't?" the man asked. "What does that mean?"

"You can go see what it means."

The man opened his car door quickly and Jimmy stepped back, nearly losing his footing.

"Son, you listen now. I don't want to offend you after your grandfather just passed, but you might go asking after your own family about what you found on your land before you come storming up here all half-cocked. You may or may not have found something down there, I don't know, I don't know anything about what's down there. But you better get talking to the rest of your family before you go calling any deputy sheriff or cussing somebody else."

"I'm going to give you until tomorrow morning to pick up your mess and then I'm going to let the sheriff come sort it out." He got in his truck and slammed the door. "I don't want to see a trace, not one single stake or collar."

"All right, hold on. Goddamn it now, hold on." The man was walking toward Jimmy when Jimmy slammed the gas to the floor. The truck lurched out of the field into the road. "Jesus!" the man yelled as he jumped away from the driver's side mirror. In the rearview Jimmy watched the man as he slowly got back to his truck, his face bright with anger. He pulled his dip from the side of his mouth and slung it out into the shoulder and stood watching Jimmy leave.

That evening Jimmy could smell the air moving through the trees, the smell of wet pine and masty scrub oak, the weather changing. He lit two gas burners on the stove with a match, two labial syllables igniting the blue halos that floated over the iron hoops. He placed a pot of water for coffee on one, over the other he rubbed his hands. When his hands warmed he began to open and shut the kitchen cabinets over the stove. Sept had left behind a handful of things: canned pears and tomatoes, some mixed dry beans. In the back of the cabinet he found black-eyed peas and ate them cold out of the can with a fork. They were salty and soft. He ate the pears after, cutting them in half in the can with the side of his fork.

He poured the coffee into Sept's old thermos and put it in a bird bag, along with a box of cartridges for the Winchester and a flashlight. He threw the Winchester across his back.

Outside, he stashed his truck down the lane of the abandoned firebreak and started off on foot down through the woods, moving quick, down to meet the road that wound its way along the hill to the back of the property where he had found the dogs. He listened to the briars whistle across his clothing and kept an ear out for the sound of an engine on the road ahead.

He arrived at the road just as light was fading in the gaps above the trees. In the woods that unspooled beside him the shadows spilled into one another. Against the faint blue light of early dark the trees retracted into slim one-dimensional cut-outs, cartoonish, looming over him like props on a stage.

Soon he found himself climbing up the backside of the earthen walls that formed the irrigation pond. There was a shallow cleft in the wall high up on the dam's rim, a good place to sit and wait. He took out the coffee thermos and spun its base a few times on the ground until it stood upright in its own footprint. He put five cartridges into the Winchester, holding it close against his body to dampen the sound as he closed the action. He sat back comfortably with the dense weight of Oct's gun across his lap and sipped his coffee.

The light was poor on the field. He couldn't make out that much at first, just the glossy drums and the silhouette of the pivot in the distance. Then the moon got up over and he could see everything well and found his position better than he thought, shaded from the moon by the trees alongside the pond, safe, unseen.

He couldn't remember falling asleep, he just knew that he woke with a pounding in his chest. The sound of a truck engine down-shifting. He looked out toward the easement road. Nothing there. The sound came from behind him, around the edge of the dam. He wasn't expecting anyone from that side. The truck must have driven right past Sept's trailer. He hadn't expected that kind of audacity. He sat up and pulled the rifle into his lap.

Headlights swung out over the field, carving out sections of darkness, forcing them into a strange and vivid life and then returning them just as suddenly to the blue night. The truck appeared, rambling slowly to where the first barrel lay, its suspension lopping in and out of the old furrows. It pulled up where the dead mastiff had been lying all afternoon, and stopped. Three men got out of the cab.

"Ain't no barking," one said.

"I can tell you why, too. Shit," the other said. His flashlight was on the mastiff. The dog's quilted fur shined in the light through the grass.

"What's that."

"Come see yerself what."

There was an older man with them. He dropped the tail-gate and lit a cigarette.

"That dog was a corpse anyway," one said.

"Got a hole here and here. What is that? .38?"

And then his great-uncle Oct's voice came across the field, some forty yards away, impossibly familiar. It was a voice almost identical to his grandfather's, the sound plunging inside him. He felt woozy. He knew the silhouette of Octavius on sight. How had he not seen him, the wisps of white hair, the slow, deliberate movements? How had he not seen him, not known him?

"It's a .22," his great-uncle said without even getting off the tailgate to see.

Jimmy examined the truck again. He had just assumed it was a green Chevy. But it was a deep navy-blue Dodge Ram, battered in the doors, rusted along the runner.

He watched them roll the truck up from drum to drum. Octavius stayed inside the truck cab while the other two men lifted the heavy animals by the legs and tossed them into the bed. They got the last dog and came back toward the pond and stopped beneath Jimmy for a moment to secure a tarp over their cargo. The dogs were piled without order, their heads and limbs facing in every direction.

He lifted the rifle and put a bead on the passenger window and sat with his hands growing slick against the stock. He laid his pointer finger gently on the side of the trigger, laid his upper cheek against the comb and eyed his great-uncle through the sight.

For a while he looked down the sight of the Winchester at his great-uncle sitting in the truck. He felt the tension in the trigger. His mind clouded up with doubts that shadowed the length of his childhood, every piece of it, obscured somehow by this moment. Had Sept not known about this? He couldn't

be certain anymore. Maybe Oct was playing his brother. Maybe
they were both involved. Maybe his grandfather knew and was
too ashamed or weak to do anything.

He pulled the rifle in tight and aimed into the hood of
the truck and exhaled and made a fist. The rifle packed itself
against his shoulder, the cartridge tumbling out of the action,
smoking in the clay. The sound was massive, hammering
across the field where it scattered into the trees. The radiator
hissed as steam poured out from under the truck's hood into
the headlights. The men dropped the tarp and scattered. One
scurried around the edge of the bed and crouched down with
his back against the tire, yelling. "Oct? My Goddamn. Oct.
Who's out there? Jesus.Who is that?"

Oct was laid down across the seat of the truck and shouting
too, "Who's out there? Who's that?" The other man had taken
off into the field, lumbering in long awkward strides over the
furrows until he vanished into the dark.

Jimmy slammed the bolt forward, clapped it down. This
time the round found the engine block and rang with a dull
thunk. He was nothing they could hope to see, encompassed
by all that darkness along the dam. They could hear only the
thunder of the Winchester as it came from above and echoed
down into the empty field. He threw the bolt again and aimed
at the right front tire. The truck's suspension knelt down into
the field as the air poured out. He shot the rear tire too so that
the truck was soon listing over to its passenger side.

He heard Oct calling his name: Jimmy Boy, Jimmy. He
shot the front windshield out from the inside, through the passenger window, heard the glass falling on the hood and that
shut his great-uncle up. Then he was running. He ran down
the steep bank and through the center of the empty irriga-

tion pond behind him, disoriented, slipping in the clay, falling knee deep into the stale water. He made his way back out to the road and kept running until his throat was raw and burning. When he made it to his truck, his back and shoulder were bruised from the rifle.

He had the accelerator to the floor halfway to the interstate until the engine ran hot and he had to back it off. He was heading north, out of Georgia, but not home. He couldn't think, couldn't decide what he would tell his father. He wouldn't. He looked down at Sept's belongings piled hurriedly on the floorboard beside him. Those things his father had asked him to bring home. He picked up the antique fishing reel and sat it in his lap. The papers and documents beneath—titles, family deeds, tract maps—levitated as the air stirred in the cab; they turned like leaves, some flying out the window, some getting pinned against the back glass.

The Strength of Fields

For James Dickey

I T IS ANOTHER EARLY WINTER MORNING. Our last name hangs in tall blue type across the side of Dad's work van: *Walker's Irrigation.* One taillight is covered in cellophane, framed in duct tape. Along the wheel well by my feet is a long rusty gash Dad calls the "trash can." It shows a sliver of the uncoiling wet road.

When I was younger this van made me proud. Other kids came to school in slick anonymous cars, their arrival unannounced by a tremendous white van bearing their last name in broadside, stalling and roaring to life again as my brother and I bailed out of it. None of that bothered me. It never once occurred to me that we didn't have another car, or that my father was a strange wreck of a person.

We're late again and Dad is accelerating through the tight bends at the bottom of Briar Creek Road. My little brother, David, sleeps in the passenger seat, his head listing left then right in his parka's hood. I'm sitting beside him on an empty spool of wire, leaning into the turns. The heater in the van broke the weekend before last, and now my brother's breath is making small clouds that hover just before his face. The light from the window inscapes them as they vanish.

"What are you thinking this morning?" Dad asks me, slapping my leg, shouting over the rattle of the gear. A copper fitting lying in the long blade of a trenching shovel rings like an alarm. Dad hands me a penny from the cupholder.

"Penny for your thoughts," he says.

"I don't know," I say. I toss the penny back into the console. Outside the passenger window, the low morning light strobes along the base of the pines as the woods thin. The window turns opaque as stone before the light sweeps off of it. Countless shutterings, the whole world growing staccato, the light, the gear, everything.

"You like that?" Dad asks me, nodding at the flickering light.

"Yeah."

"You're gonna make yourself carsick."

"I'm all right," I say.

"That light," he says, licking his lips, and I can tell he has a real doozy coming. "That's God," he says, "knocking on your door, knocking with his Sunday knucks."

"Knucks?"

"Yeah, knucks." He makes a fist and taps me on the top of my skull. I take his hand and hold it in my lap and count the months across his big knucks like they taught us in school. I remember the short ones and the long ones, I remember February and look to see if that notch is somehow shallower than the others. God is light, I think. And the light is knocking on me with its Sunday knucks, and some of the knucks have thirty days and some have thirty-one, so that a year has a tide, so that everything is knocking on the world. How strangely insistent and intrusive, my father's percussive God.

His expressions were always that way. Inviting as a maze. I learned to hold his words the way you hold a cricket in your palm. I would think about them later, long and hard like a kid does. I would part the fingers of my mind and peek at that strange and fragile thing and wonder about it, try hard not to lose or disfigure it, but that is inevitably what happens.

"You're kind as kindling," he would say, one of my favorites—and that one is tricky, you see, because it plays off the appearance of the words, not the sound—or, "You've got a heart like pine, Mr. Turpentine." He was warm that way, always tender, and maybe that's the worst part. He had such a capacity to draw me in, and yet what was he drawing me in to exactly? What did it amount to, his tenderness? Is tenderness everything? Will tenderness inherit the earth?

I was thinking about all this at work, thinking about those rides in the early morning to school, the shiver of milk-pale light, the smell of pipe glue and solvent flooding my clothing, my hair, worrying my teachers. I was running through it over and over again like it was a problem that needed solving. Could I figure it out? Figure out when and what happened inside my father's head? If I assembled all the clues, could I then? I couldn't. I knew that and yet my mind, my memories, seemed bent on trying.

More often now I have begun to think about something my mother said once about Dad. I remember we were standing in the kitchen and it was early on a Saturday morning. I was pulling down the lids to all the pots and pans, and she was stowing them under the cabinet, where she could get to them. Dad had moved to Florida earlier that week to spend a month living with his brother. We didn't know then that he wasn't coming back.

"I don't know why he put them up there so high," she said.

"Yeah, who knows," I said, reaching up, but even I was barely tall enough. My fingertips crawled along the lids to the handles. I handed them down one by one.

"I just don't know him," she said, as if I weren't even in the room, as if the thought had just then occurred to her. "I don't know anything about him."

"Yeah, you do." I said. "He's just not himself. It'll be all right."

"No," she said. "He has *never* been himself."

I drove the long way home, down Old Horrel Hill Road, where the trees are heavy-limbed and when you move out from the brakes the fields are suddenly there, stretching out all around you, brooding their strength and warmth. Peanuts and cotton come in at the start of fall; driving past makes the low-hunched rows flash. Run the car faster and the cotton blurs like snow. My father would have something great for this, I thought. He would say something to tumble my mind out the truck window, send me spinning into the brambles.

I imagined what it would be like when I got home that evening, felt my foot ease off the gas. No need to hurry. My little brother would be downstairs, cross-legged on the floor, playing a video game. Mom would be in the kitchen, putting something together for dinner, exhaustion hanging on her like a weight, like you could just tip her right over. Strange meals lately: black-eyed peas and scrambled eggs. Frozen waffles and salad.

The house would be dark, the lights she forgot to turn on, blinds she forgot to shut, trash she forgot to take out, my brother's clothing and notebooks lining one side of the stairs, the wheels coming off our domestic life. Would it have been like this if Dad hadn't gone down to Florida? Could any of us have seen it coming, seen the fissure inside his mind like a crack in a windshield? I imagine my father's head full of these expanding shapes, complex, crystalline. They are the crazy stories he tells us at night before bed; they are the greasy diagnostic paths of an automotive manual; they are the mad genes my brother and I share, in every cell of our bodies.

Mom and I pooled our work money the summer Dad moved out. I dropped out of college and left my apartment. I've been at home now almost three years. The arrangement was supposed to be for only a year, to help Mom with David, to get us back on our feet. And then David was suddenly a teenager and started getting into trouble and Mom wanted me around. Most recently, he was caught at school with a box cutter and got suspended for two weeks. Two weeks of counseling appointments during the day, so that Mom has to take off work to get him there.

"I forgot to take it out of my backpack," he said to me. But I knew where that cutter came from. We all knew. It was in the cupholder of Dad's work van for years; it has Dad's initials gouged into one side. I don't know when he got it out of the van or how long he's had it. Even hearing about it made me want to see it again. I wanted to heft the heavy cutter, feel those carved initials under my thumb. I like to think David was using it to open something and just held onto it. Or that he missed

Dad and wanted it with him at school. I like to think Dad didn't give it to him as a parting gift.

Near home, on the new four-lane highway, car dealerships have gathered. When my parents moved out here there was nothing, a small blacktop road, a gas station, poultry and horse farms. Now bright, mad acetylene lights burn all night over the glossy automotive fields, blotting out the stars. The mental health hospital is on the other side of the road from the dealership. All night long the dealership lights gleam in the madness of the razor wire. Large violent curls, beautiful and intricate, hang in bobs up the tall, inverted parabola, and it makes you wonder, seeing all that razor wire, seeing it shine all night long, just who is living in there, and why all that fuss, and what would they do to you if they met you on the street. Would they say warm, strange things to you? Would they tuck you in, hand you the gift of a story, an old knife, kiss your forehead softly like a mother?

Darkness was lowering slowly over the county, pressing the light down into the earth. I thought of the orange glow of medication bottles surrounding my father these days like a shrine: muscle relaxers, antianxiety meds, sleep meds, allergy meds for the allergies he never had. And where did he get all this stuff? What doctor would write him these prescriptions—he, who was living in Florida in my Uncle Eric's room over the garage. He, who believed suddenly he was sick with something, believed my mother was poisoning him, and then cheating on him.

I was sixteen when it started. It was insane, and for a few months he drew me into it with him. I remember waiting for Dad outside the doctor's office and worrying with him, being sorry he was sick, hoping the doctors would just give him a diagnosis. And then I watched Mom with his suspicion; I tried it on like an oversized coat. Could Mom have someone? Was it possible that she needed that?

And then, after a few months, I realized it wasn't real, it couldn't be, not any of it. Mom had no one but us. And Dad's disorders shifted shape too quickly and seemed paired to his Internet search history. The realization of these facts was a kind of relief to me, relief like the strange wavelength of light that accompanies the beautiful and profound silence one encounters in the eye of a hurricane.

I opened the front door that evening to find Mom pulling all the cushions off the sofa. She didn't look up. She moved on to the love seat and threw those cushions onto the others.

"Blanket fort?" I asked.

"David's missing. I can't find my keys."

She stirred the contents of her purse for several seconds and then dumped the entire thing onto the coffee table. Scraps of papers, a tremendous bottle of ibuprofen, all sorts of trash. No keys.

"I think he might have my keys."

"Why would he have your keys?"

"I don't know. I slapped him."

"God, Mom."

"I know."

"When?"

"After he got off the bus. A few hours ago."

We got in my truck and drove to the McDonald's across the road from our subdivision. The place was all windows, vivid with light.

"He's not here," I said.

"Just go check. Check in the bathroom."

I went in and he wasn't there. When I got back Mom was crying pretty hard.

"We'll find him," I said.

"I know," she said.

When we first moved to this neighborhood the only home besides ours was the model home at the entrance. We didn't realize it then but it meant that my brother and I would grow up surrounded by construction sites, piles of mortar sand, the sharp report of unloaded lumber, men crowding around fire barrels in the early winter morning, air compressors hissing, the constant snap of the roofers' and framers' nail guns. The suburbs in a state of infancy, the felling of long-leaf pines, the backdrop of our childhood.

Of course we played in those unfinished houses every day after school when the workers pulled out. We played in them all weekend long. We examined their trash and tools. We knew the bitter smell of drywall mud and the sweetness of sawdust in the hot summer. We knew the magazines we might find stashed back in the woods near their latrines, the women in those magazines with the tremendous breasts, their faces powerfully agonized, a strange invitation we barely understood. We knew the spaces between bare studs, knew we could run through them without slowing down. We knew these things as if they were ours, an extension of our own home.

I thought my brother would be inside one of those houses. I could see him sitting in an unpainted room, watching the rectangular light shapes shift and bend along the wall as cars passed down the road, and listening to the sound of wind whistling through the uncaulked gaps above the window's keeper rail.

So I drove to the back of the subdivision, where the few last homes were still unfinished. Mom was calming down some. I rubbed her back.

"What happened?" I asked.

"He got written up his first day back. I told him not to smile at me or I'd slap it off his face."

"Jesus, Mom."

"I know," she said.

"What was the write-up?"

"Mr. McCance asked him to stand during class."

"Was he falling asleep?"

"I don't know."

"He wouldn't stand?"

"I guess not."

I took the house on the left, Mom the one on the right. The front doors were installed and locked. I jumped down from the porch and headed around to the back. There was no porch there, just a long two-by-eight plank as a ramp that ran to an open door about eight feet off the ground. I could see tracks there, fresh orange clay up the plank. I followed the tracks into the house, across the kitchen tiles, and then up the rosewood stairs, each imprint growing fainter and fainter until disappearing in the powder of drywall dust. When I got to the top, I turned, following the faintest impression in the dust into a bathroom.

David was sitting there on the toilet seat, looking at me with his wide eyes, huge green-rimmed holes. The mirror over the sink was bashed in several places. The window beside the toilet was missing some panes. Blood was in the dry sink and on his pants, blood blossoming through his coat pocket where he'd shoved his right hand.

"How long you been in here?" I asked.

"Mom's being a huge bitch," he said and started tearing up, his mouth unstable.

"Yeah, I heard."

"I hate that bitch," he said.

"She's real upset."

"Good."

"How bad is your hand?"

"I don't know."

"What happened at school?"

"Nothing. Dad called."

"Dad called? He called you at school?"

"Yeah."

The broken glass in the window seemed to wheeze, as if the house were trying to breathe through the fissures. The sound of wind in the pines out back.

"What did he say?"

"He said he was real sick and stuff and wanted to see us."

"You know he isn't sick, though, not in that way?"

"Yeah, I know."

"Does that water run? You should run your hand in it."

I tried the tap. Got nothing. The blood in the sink looked purple now in the dim light. I thought I could smell it in the room, the iron oxidizing.

"Come on," I said. "It's too cold to stay in here."

We came down together and found Mom sitting in the driver's seat of my truck. I got in the back of the bed and David got in behind me.

"Ride up front," I said.

"I don't want to talk to her."

"Ride up front."

"You ride up front," he said.

Mom got out and leaned on the bed rail and looked at us sitting together in the bed. David sat with his back against the cab, and pocketed his hands. He did not look at her.

"I'll never do that again," she said to him.

He stared at his shoes.

"Did you hear?" I asked.

He clicked the toes of his boots.

"He cut his hand on some glass," I said. "We should probably go to the doc-in-a-box."

"Can I see it? David, sweetie? Can I see it?" Mom reached to pull the hand out of his pocket and he swatted her hand away with his good one.

"Let's just go home," he said.

She stood for a moment, wanting him to look at her, and then she gave up and got in the driver's seat.

We lay down with our backs against the bed liner and saw the streetlights of our subdivision pass overhead, each a wild system of moth life. We passed our house. We passed the dealerships and the grocery stores and the doc-in-a-box. We passed the exit for the hospital. We passed everything and she kept going and David and I looked at each other and smiled and said nothing. We watched the constellations clarify outside the city. The smell of fertilizer hung in the cooling fields. If this was her gift to us we took it. We guessed at where we were, guessed at the whole world sliding by. The limbs of oak trees vaulted over us, the wide and single stars, ever increasing.

I thought of David's hand in his bloody pocket and wondered how bad it was. I wondered what Dad said to him on the phone. I thought of David's wildness, wild to be wreckage forever. My brother had knocked on his own reflection like a god; like a god he made the image inscrutable. The truck downshifted, and we stopped asking ourselves where she was going. We stopped asking for anything.

Stretch Out Your Hand

I SAW THE FEVER AS IT LEFT HER BODY. It swam out of the ends of her hair, silent as heat lightning. So many long strands of light—each hair casting off something that looked like silk until the filaments were thin and lucent. They rose from Ruth's head and gathered in the joists of the ceiling. A bright, glowing nest.

My father raised her up, walking in small orbits between the bed and the open door, bobbing her in his arms. "Ruth?" he asked, "can you hear me?" She seemed to wake for a moment and then fell soundly back asleep.

Her fever had stayed on for a little more than three weeks, nearly a month in all, coming in waves but never breaking. Toward the end of that month it seemed an inseparable part of her, like her voice or her inattention to detail. *And then, gone?* But it wasn't gone because I could see it, hanging in the room above us—a nest of light that swam out of her hair and hung itself in the ceiling joists as if it were waiting for us to leave so it might descend. Not gone at all, but dazzling—suspended over us. *How could they not see it? Shouldn't we turn down the light and open a window? Is a fever like a bird? Or a moth?*

"She needs rest," my mother said.

"Ruth?" my father said again.

"She's not going anywhere," my mother said. She took the girl and laid her back down on the mattress. "We will try some food in the morning. Some toast and broth."

"Benjamin," my father said, "please go and get your sister some more water. *Cold* water, please."

Sickness can show you things, things you have acknowledged time and again and yet, in a more mysterious way, never recognized. And which of these things is more miraculous: the incandescent movement of my sister's fever, or the way my father held her? I can't say. There is a place in me where these things go. My envy goes there and works in ways I can't imagine, as does my fear. I can feel these things meeting in this place, like groundwater converging, but I can never hear or make sense of what is being said. I have no idea what goes on in there.

I opened the back door and stepped down onto the path to the well. Fall was coming on slowly. It had been a fine summer starting out, but now the entire season was overshadowed. Across the two-acre garden the Brysons' windows were lit, and the light spilled through the gaps between the dogwoods, producing large vascular shapes along the ground.

August 1924 pressed its heat directly into us; it entered our bodies like flukes that spin unseen in river water, determined to stay. Though the season would change and winter would eventually come, the vegetables in their jars on the basement floor would be brought up from the cellar and relished—the sweet pickled okra, the brine-kept cabbage and turnips—this summer and the fevers it brought with it would never leave. Not for us and especially not for the Brysons.

My eyes were trying to fix on the dim outline of the well pump in the dark, though it was too far away just yet to be seen. I kept my eyes leveled out on the darkness. I stayed where the path was packed hard beneath my feet and if I felt the path grow soft on one side or another I turned back to the center.

Things had been suspended for weeks. Every movement had Ruth's bed at its center and now that I was out again, standing in the cool evening, I felt like walking until I couldn't walk anymore. I felt like standing out there away from that room, away from everything, looking back at the house from an invisible point in the shadow of the tree line. There was a freedom in knowing that I could be found only if I wanted to be. The blue-rimmed reflection of the moon on the iron pump handle began to appear in front of me, and then a small circle shining up from the reservoir beneath.

I dropped the bucket into the barrel half-buried in the ground under the pump spout. I pushed the bucket half beneath the surface of the standing water, feeling the upward pressure it gave in return. I moved the bucket below the pump and flipped its handle on top of the spout, and when it was secure I took the pump's arm and began to raise the water.

My older sister was away at college in Salt Lake City, two days' train ride from Dyersburg. She and Ruth were never playmates. For Ruth, Hannah was just another extension of our mother. Eight years older than me and fourteen years older than Ruth,

Hannah was the overseer of chores. She took after our father, and in that way she could be impenetrable and distant. Even when we were young she was always about some business of her own, allowing interruption only to see to something my mother asked of her, like setting the table.

There were times when I would let myself believe that Hannah and my father were trying to appeal to Ruth and me through their reticence, as if we should expect to find in their stoicism some secret inclination of their affections, and I would look for these moments the way someone might watch a statue for a long time with an uncanny mixture of both apprehension and desire, to see if it might wink or smile. I know that Ruth and I shared this fantasy. We waited and kept faith with it, believing that our father was not cold but some-how wise, and that he had schemed an elaborate game by which he always did the opposite of what he felt, and that this was for our benefit in a way we couldn't understand because we were young.

Ruth's only real playmate was the neighbors' little girl. They called her Sam. She had six older brothers and, like Ruth, was lanky and curious about everything. Sam wasn't allowed to attend school the year Ruth started. At my mother's insistence my father paid Mr. Bryson a visit. One evening after dinner, I pretended to square up the woodpile as my mother buried some potatoes beneath the back porch. Over our shoulders we watched as my father cut through the brake and visited Mr. Bryson on his front porch.

They spoke for only twenty minutes, and I don't know what my father said exactly, but the next day Sam and Ruth, arm in arm, were off to downtown Dyersburg. Sam even had a lunch packed for her in a little lavender-colored sling she wore over her shoulder. They walked in front of me, talking very seriously and quietly for two seven-year-old girls.

After that afternoon the two were as indivisible as a dovetail joint. Sam and Ruth dealt peaceably with school and books and were not bad students, but it was in the long Tennessee summers that they prospered. Their skin darkened together. They came into the house smelling of hay or creek water. From time to time they were forced to play with the younger of Sam's brothers, but more often they would disappear together into the tree line down the hill from the house, reemerging with their hems soaked and muddy, carrying crawdads in their dresses that they lifted out away from their stomachs to form pockets where the pink, brittle creatures squirmed and rolled on top of each other.

Late in their fourth summer together, they each came down with fevers.

Mr. Bryson ran a small dairy, about thirty Holsteins in all. A few of Sam's brothers had started giving the girls milk from time to time. It had been going on for weeks.

"Weeks!" Mr. Bryson said in front of my father and mother, as if to sound surprised that such behavior could happen on his property.

The older boys knew they weren't allowed to drink raw milk, the younger ones too, but they didn't know why. It was prohibited and for that reason sensuous. The girls would lift the hefty pails up to their faces and take long drafts, each helping the other not spill. The milk was warm and heavy with fat. It ran down their cheeks and necks, into their shirt collars. It felt as if they were crossing some threshold together, and then it felt as if they were filling themselves up with the summer itself. All of it, every lavish thing, inseparable.

The inside throat of the aluminum pail would be scalloped with cloudy white layers, each tress a sediment that signified their trespasses. They pressed their tongues against the roofs of their mouths to feel the sleek residue while they patted the Holsteins' sweat-smelling flanks and stared into the wet globes of those eyes that were much larger than their own and just as near to panic as compliance as the boys pulled aggressively on the udders. Streams of milk hissed against the edge of the half-full pail, ringing it, the pitch rising higher and higher as it filled.

Sam was first. Mr. Bryson came over and told my mother that Sam had a bad fever. I remember that he didn't even come all the way up the porch steps. He stood on the second step with his hand on the rail, swatting his hat against his leg, looking down to where the rail met the column—as if he were inspecting it. He said he thought the boys had been giving the girls raw milk. He ran his hand across his bald head, which was very red and wet with sweat. My mother thanked him and went immediately to Ruth, who was pulling sheets from the line out back and doing a terrible job of folding them, before stacking them on the grass instead of putting them in her basket. Mother let the back door smack closed behind her and approached Ruth so quickly and with such a serious expression that Ruth dropped her sheet unfolded in a clump at her feet and began to back away as if retreating from an assault. Mother snatched her by the arm and drew Ruth in between her legs. She laid her hand across Ruth's brow and after a long pause dropped to one knee and with her thumbs pulled down the skin below Ruth's eyes and peered hard into each one.

"What, Momma?" Ruth asked.

Three times during dinner my mother reached across the table and cupped the side of Ruth's face with her palm. She gave her extra water. Eventually Father asked Ruth if she had been drinking milk at the Brysons', and Ruth said, "No, sir," and then after a moment, "Yes, sir." He told Ruth that Sam was sick, that perhaps one of the cows was sick too, and that she was not to visit her until they gave permission.

Ruth sat very quiet for the rest of the meal. We tried not to stare at her. Mother ate quickly and took my plate before I was finished. Then we watched Ruth eat her greens and drink her water. We watched her as if she might suddenly combust. She chewed deliberately and rocked back and forth some in her chair, her legs kicking beneath the table.

Later that evening Ruth asked if she could listen to the radio. Again, my mother held her face for a long time and finally she said, "Only a few minutes." Ruth fell asleep that night on the carpet, listening to a recording we had heard a number of times that year of George Gershwin playing "Rhapsody in Blue" at the Aeolian Hall.

The next morning Ruth sat down beside me at the table and I could feel the warmth coming off her skin. I felt it through my shirt.

"Ruth?" I said. I reached out to touch her arm. The skin seemed to swell beneath my hand. Her eyes were dim, the skin around them an unusual gray. My mother didn't even turn around. She wiped her hands on her apron, set a skillet on the stove top, filled it with water, and pulled a handful of willow bark from the cabinet above her. She dropped the bark into the skillet and stirred it some, and then removed a glass jar from the shelf over the range and, filling it halfway with water, added some sugar with a spoon and began to stir. She was careful and deliberate and Ruth and I watched her, spellbound.

A chain of events, their particular order laid out by my mother, their contingencies and variations known only to her—as this was her true gift—was now in motion. Once the skillet came to a boil, she took the handsaw off the shelf over the icebox, went out to the barn, brushed the sawdust off the block of ice, and removed a perfect and large triangle of ice from one corner—an action I would have been reprimanded for by my father, as ice was to be taken off only in cubes, requiring three separate cuts, and the sawdust then shoveled back on top of the ice. Rules of this sort were always kept; that they could be so quickly discarded was scandalous to me.

My mother had the piece of ice in a big pail on the kitchen table before the screen door had a chance to slap closed behind her. She threw a washrag over her shoulder and filled the pail with water, saying, "Ruth, go to your room and take off your clothes. Lay them across your foot chest . . . neatly, please." She poured the boiling water into the jar with the sugar water and stirred. The concoction was an off-brown haze, clouded like disturbed pond water. She stuck the foggy willow bark mixture into the icebox and disappeared down the hallway with ice pail and rag in hand.

This was the beginning of my mother's reign over the movements of our household. My father and I became extensions of her limbs, every movement aimed with an unbelievable persistence at Ruth's recovery. We retrieved ice. We heated broth. We washed Ruth's sheets. My father still went to work at the mill but came home during lunch. I prepared meals.

After two days, with neither fever lifting in our house or the Brysons', I was woken early in the morning. A voice, a person I couldn't see in the dark, told me to walk to the Bobbits' house and to ask to use their phone. If they were home, I was to call the doctor in from Jonesboro; if they weren't, I was to go on to the Gowans'. I walked out in the dim morning with the feeling that I was in a war, carrying a vital message from one general to another. I cut through the Fleshmans' soy to get out to the main road just as the light was coming up, drawing out its long shadows through the furrows. I slipped under the Fleshmans' wire fence and stepped onto the road. The dew on the high grass in the spine of the road wet my shoes and the cuffs of my pants.

Mrs. Bobbit already knew about the two girls. She met me at the door, her large body filling the entryway, and said, "You need to call? This way, sweetie." The doctor came that evening and visited Sam first, at my mother's insistence, and then Ruth. I watched as he extended Ruth's arm out beside her. He laid two fingers softly on her wrist and stared for a long time at his watch. He pressed on her stomach in many places with his fingertips until Ruth shifted and let out a little moan.

While my mother and the doctor went into the kitchen I sat on the edge of Ruth's bed and showed her my penny trick. I held the penny in my right hand with both of my hands extended out and open. I heard my mother offering the doctor coffee.

"Enlarged liver," he said.

I flipped my hands over, carefully moving the penny from one hand to the other.

"Malta fever. It comes in waves." he said.

"Willow aspirin?" my mother asked.

"It won't help."

I showed Ruth my closed fists. "Which one?" I asked her.

One morning, a week after the doctor's first visit, all six of
the Bryson boys were sitting outside in the shade, leaning with
their backs against the side of their house. They were wearing
undershirts and pants but no work shirts. A few of them stared
in my direction; two had their arms crossed, their heads hanging down toward the dirt, and the youngest was tearing a leaf
in half and throwing the strips out between his legs.

They were disheveled and sleepy, not one of them saying a word. I couldn't remember ever seeing them all in one
place before, much less sitting *still* in one place. Not even in
church were they so still, and the sight of them made me feel
empty. I had to force myself to start walking again, to try to
remember where I was going or what I was doing, and then
suddenly I understood. I turned to them, and they looked
back at me, and I could suddenly hear it, and I knew.

A terrible sound came from inside their house, and then
it seemed to be coming not just from their house but from
all directions, hanging in the tree limbs like buzzards. Mrs.
Bryson was screaming, crying in long intervals as if she were
in labor, and all the boys wore a look of torment on their
faces. Each time she screamed their faces twisted and churned
beneath the pressure of the sound.

I left the ice pail and the handsaw sitting in the middle
of our yard and ran to the back door. My hand failed twice at
the knob before I opened the door. I went to find my mother.
She was bathing Ruth. My sister's thin, nude body was laid

out on the bed like a corpse, and I couldn't take my eyes from
it. I realized then that the door to her room had been shut
and that I hadn't knocked. The small, thin patch of pubic
hair where her legs met shined like dull copper, and I stared
at the place. The hip bones were broader than I would have
thought, more feminine, steeped out above the low curve of
her pelvis and the mound that rose softly there. I'd never
seen her nude, not since she was a baby. Was this her body?
She was gaunt, always, but never so slight. Her tiny arms, wet
from the washrag, seemed impossibly narrow. Her ribs were
larger than I imagined and protruded out beside her small
breasts. Her skin flushed still with heat.

My mother drew the sheet over her, up to her neck, a movement that unlocked my gaze. I had forgotten myself. *Alive*, I
thought. *Who was screaming?* I felt my knees buckle. The room
throbbed. The sight of those six boys in their white undershirts
came back to me, the horrible sound.

"Benjamin?" my mother asked.

I gripped the door frame but found my grip too weak to
hold me. I grew dizzy. A dark tunnel formed. At the end of the
tunnel my mother sat on the edge of the bed beside my sister.
It was suddenly far below me. I was on my knees, holding the
door frame but feeling as though I were about to fall down into
the opening. *Dead? No, alive.* What was it that I needed to say?
What was it I saw and heard? And then the thought came, not
like a word but like a breath knocked out of me.

"Sam . . . I think Sam is . . ." I said.

And before the words were completely out, my mother had
me, her hand over my mouth. She was turning my body gently but with more composure and strength than I would have
thought possible for her size. I was lying now on my side in the

doorway with her hand, cold and smelling of lake ice, over my mouth.

"Hush. Hush. Hush," she said.

My father and mother went to pay a short visit to the Brysons that evening. Mother wore a brown dress with dark red lace around the sleeves and the collar, my father his black suit. Earlier that afternoon my mother prepared a stew for their family, enough for the six boys. She cut the carrots and potatoes in large chunks because her hands were so unsteady. She trembled as she cleaned the chickens. And now, as she held the heavy stew in the only nice dish we owned, a large white pot with a big wide lid and blue flowers on the sides, I noticed that she could barely stand. Fear was astounding us, its full power arriving and astonishing. We were learning, as a family, all the ways that fear could force the mind into painful and unstable positions. My father took the pot of stewed chicken from my mother and led her across the garden and then carefully up the Brysons' front steps.

Sam, who was shorter than Ruth by a few inches but had the same dark-brown hair, was laid out on the kitchen table in her white church dress. The coroner still hadn't come. It didn't make sense for her to be where she was. Why not in her room? Maybe they couldn't stand that room. Mrs. Bryson accepted the pot of stew from my father. Her hair, a tangle of wisps, some silver and some still the palest blonde, surrounded her swollen face, her eyes like nickel slots. She put the pot down on the floor by her feet and then, realizing her mistake, brought it near the table and turned around suddenly and put it on a shelf in the living room as if it were a decoration.

My parents couldn't even look at Sam. They couldn't speak. It was Mrs. Bryson who finally said, "We're so sorry. The boys just didn't know no better. They just didn't know." And my mother shook her head back and forth violently, her eyes wide, as if to say, "Stop, stop," because she needed to reject the apology, needed to deny the idea implicit in Mrs. Bryson's words.

I stayed beside Ruth that evening, waiting for the rag that lay over her neck to grow warm, waiting to wring it out and replace it with another, which lay cooling in the ice water by my feet. Beads of water condensed on the sides of the galvanized metal bucket, then gathered the smaller beads hanging beneath them to run in long streaks down the bucket's side. As I moved the wash pail closer to the bed, it left wet rings on the unfinished pine floor, each slightly eccentric to the one beside it, as if someone had been drafting a circle freehand, tightening each orbit to achieve a closer form.

At the funeral service the minister preached on a passage from John's Gospel. He was a young man, tall and thin with dark curly hair and a fierce sort of expression, the kind of minister who takes himself too seriously but only because of his nervousness. My mother and I attended together while my father stayed with Ruth. I now know that Momma must have longed desperately—even needed—to leave that service. She neither cried nor spoke as she listened to the sermon.

"We must, in these times," the young man said, "not be as Thomas, who doubted the Resurrection, and of whom our Lord had said, 'Stretch out your hand and put it here in my side; and be not unbelieving but believing.'" The minister then looked up toward the Brysons and appeared to forget his point. He took a moment again to find his place in the text, and in the silence it seemed suddenly clear that nothing could be said for this. After what seemed to me a very long time the man finally continued, "As our Lord said to Thomas, 'Blessed are they who have not seen and yet have believed.' Let us pray."

It was certain. Ruth was a day late contracting the fever, and she would be a day late passing. We were waiting. I knew if my mother prayed, it was not in the hopes of some unseen place but in strident hope against it. My mother was a woman for whom seeing *was* believing, who, without the slightest contrition, would have proudly stretched out her hand.

For the Brysons death was plain and physical; it came before they knew to fear it. For us it became something worse. It lingered; its sour stench pulsated inside our house, its presence embodied in a single word: *milk*. Our minds tried to move away from it, but fear had a hold on the words that formed our thoughts; it drew them slowly back to that single word. At the front gate, when the breeze turned toward the house and the trees hissed, I could hear it clearly, moving with the gate, over and over again: "Milk. Milk. Milk." Grief circled us, nervous, waiting to land.

After Sam died, my mother stopped sleeping in her own room. Her lips moved almost imperceptibly in prayer, even during brief moments of sleep in the small corner chair. Every time she awoke, she did so with a jerk, as if the entire house had gone over a bump in the road, and she would look to the bed as if she expected to find it empty, as if Ruth could have been jolted out of her bed and fallen down through a crack in the floor, never to be seen again.

When my mother went to the edge of Ruth's bed to take her temperature she approached very slowly, as if to give the fever warning of her approach. Then she would stand for hours at a time with her hand stuck to the side of Ruth's face, shifting her weight unconsciously between her feet, often with her eyes closed and at other times staring vacantly out the window.

A week passed this way. The fever no longer came in waves but stayed on steady and hot.

And then one evening in late August, my mother woke to feel a new and different breeze in the room. It was the soft movement of the fever—invisible to my parents—drifting up toward the ceiling.

I don't know if Ruth was supposed to follow Sam into that place, a place where fevers don't swim out of your hair but instead lift you up and away into some other—and more indistinct—brightness. We hadn't yet had a chance to tell the Brysons. And what would we say to them? Should we wait until Ruth was well enough to appear out in the garden or running or carrying water like a ghost?

The bucket was now half full. I lifted the handle off the spigot and set the pail on the ground by my feet. I lowered my face deep into the barrel. The barrel was full to the head hoop, and as I continued, as I lowered my shoulders, the water spilled over the lip of the chime and into the grass. I felt it run between my toes and chill the wet dirt beneath my feet. I lowered myself again, this time all the way to my chest, the water-line moving up to the middle of my stomach. I extended my arms down into the bottom of the cylinder and felt the barrel's slick staves with my hands.

I took off my wet shirt and pressed my face into it and held it there for a long time. I balled it up and pressed it up against my cheek.

I walked around in little circles beside the well, holding my shirt in my arms.

I lifted the pail of water from the ground and imagined it full of warm milk. I took several long gulps. Over the house, the glowing nest of my sister's fever drifted up into the night until it dispersed into limitless points of light that were each swallowed like spent stars against the dark vault.

I carried the fresh water into the house and set it down on the kitchen table. My mother and father were talking quietly in the living room. I stood in the entrance to the hallway for a moment, waiting to see if they would look up at me, and they did not. I went to Ruth and leaned over her bed. A few drops of water fell from my hair onto her pillow and the pattern of down emerged through the linen. I kissed Ruth on the edge of her mouth and waited to see if she would wake. When she didn't, I moved my mouth over hers again and kissed her bottom lip, holding it for a moment between my own. Her lips were cool and tasted bitter, like boiled willow.

Anchor Tree Passing

THEY CAME DOWN TO SPARTA from Blacksburg, Virginia, looking eager and mislaid. The man had the bill of sale from his father's tract in Blacksburg tucked in the front pocket of his shirt. Often as they drove he brought his hand up to his chest to feel its outline, to make sure it was real. On the far side of the road a good stand of hardwoods fell off toward a stream which ran silver-skinned and silent across the floor of the woods below. It followed them for miles, or they followed it, and he found it hard to keep his eyes on the road because of its presence.

The Freedman's Bureau and Reconstruction meant chaos; the state of Georgia was like a bushel of apples brought out to market and turned on its side, whatever could be recollected wouldn't sell for half what it might have cost if the thing hadn't spilled to begin with. Of the landowners still alive most couldn't pay the taxes and so the land went back to the state in one big pile and ended up in sheriff's auctions. Many of the big tracts were divided immediately, some set aside for freedman tenancy and some for sale. From the road these abandoned tracts—their rotund fields rising and falling away in succession—appeared like conquered giants, large slain things left on their backs in the sun, showing their swollen and furrowed underbellies.

Zachariah rode between the fields, noticing always the empty slave quarters and ginny houses. Often a door would hang open facing the road. The dark apertures, the tremendous emptiness of those places, the way the dust drifted down into the openings and then disappeared as it left the light—it all put a queer feeling inside him. He felt something sentinel there, something absorbed in that darkness, as if the openings needed to be watched to keep at bay whatever they contained. Only when they were far behind him would the feeling lift and he would remember his eagerness to see how far his money would go. He was young and he felt a pained expectancy to become, at once, all the thousands of things that seemed possible. Later in his life, after he had chipped away all the probability of himself until there was only he, himself, and no one else, he would remember this day and the horrible impatience inside him to become something he did not yet know was impossible: a proud and content man.

As they passed through Harlem the wagon went easy. He saw the wheels making smooth incisions in the land as it curled up and away. He thought of Abram sitting out that long night between the halves of his own animals, scurrying off buzzards like a man pushed beyond reason, pushed into something he couldn't understand, hoping his covenant with God would not become carrion.

His wife Katie was quiet and fiercely attentive, but not with a sense of wonder or expectation. She was five months pregnant and intent on being as still as possible. She was desperate to have a place to lie down, to be out of sight and, above all, longing for home.

She was marking the landscape at each milestone, remembering the turns, keeping track of how they came. She remembered the small county road they shifted to in Warren, the turn before that in Dearing where they followed alongside the railroad for half a day, and before that the larger well-maintained road that came down to the Hamburg landing where they crossed the Savannah. There was a burnt-out tree there. Farther along, before Abbeville in Carolina, there was a stone bridge that looked like the opening of a church door. She kept all of these carefully in her mind in case she needed to find her way back home; she was accumulating a map and tracking her place along it. When they arrived Zachariah headed inside a small courthouse and then found a place for them to stay and she rehearsed her map, wondering how long it would take her to get home if they turned right then, at that very moment, how long, how many days, if they started now.

He spent the following day with a lawyer down from Pennsylvania who worked under the Reconstruction Act. Like subjugators, they pored over a map recently revised in dark red ink. The new red lines ran in unusually square grids, hatch marks above the old lines that were far fewer and took their shape from the land itself, from its rivers, the invisible veins of clay, the water table, the vast hornblende deposits, the concerns of farmers. None of these things were taken into account on the new map. The lines went formally over these boundaries and mysteries, cutting through history, through time, through ancient stone like gods. Some of the new squares were marked in the corner with an x for tenancy, and others with a money sign for sale. The largest piece available in Sparta was off the old Terrell plantation, of which Zachariah bought seven hundred acres, four hundred of timber and three hundred cleared.

He went that evening to see the land and came to stand beneath a knotted and hardy anchor tree in the middle of the field nearest to the road. The tree bore deep circular scars in the bark on its lower trunk, crumpled places where Terrell's men had cabled the winch around it and used it to pull the other trees free of the soil. He thought of the men that came before him. He saw them standing in the same field fifty years ago, a team of sweat-salted mules yoked in a circle, tightening a heavy cable between the large tree and the surrounding stumps until the entire field was cleared, leaving this one tremendous pecan all on its own. It held its solitude up before the world like a sign. And if there had been another tree in range of the cable and if that tree would have been large enough, it too would have been cut down and its stump winched free. But there was not another tree, and so the pecan remained, a vessel of grace when the others had been destroyed. And graceful it was, with a full healthy crown in good proportion to its trunk, an exclamation in its posture there, a kind of leaving joy.

Zachariah had his heart full of cotton from the moment he crossed the Savannah. It was big money, people said, now that the planters and overseers had been taken out of the picture. The demand was high and the small farmers of the Allegheny and Appalachians, men like Zachariah who had never owned a slave, men who had barely survived a rich man's war, came south and were not averse to hiring labor and sharecroppers. They let the freedmen come and work in families, not gangs. It was their time. The scales had shifted; the lines had fallen in new and pleasant places.

The desire to prosper grew steadily in Zachariah from the moment he arrived. He stepped off the road and onto his tract and he felt something more complete and purposeful than joy: he felt a sense of power, a hunger, and he did not know that this hunger was the same hunger of Terrell and all the men before him, those men he despised. His heart had formed a tough shell around the cotton boll and it hardened the more he thought of his great chance.

Their only child, Thaddeus William Shockley, was born in late August of that year. It had been a summer of heat like they had never known, heat that permeated everything, heat that hid in the shade like a snake and stayed on through the night. But now the rain came almost every evening and when it left the first hint of fall would follow. That cool light air in late evening, and the strange long shadows of August, was like a spell or a song; it could put you to sleep. The light especially caused the mind to slow and reflect.

Katie listened to the rain dying out and tried to remember her childhood, but with Thaddeus in her lap she felt cut off from that time, as if a door had closed softly behind her and sealed perfectly into the wall. The girl she had understood herself to be was on the other side of that door, where her entire childhood lay like a dream, and she—someone now called a "mother," a name wholly strange and warm to her—was on this new side of everything, living with her husband

and child in a small Georgia town where she knew no one. Impossible that she was here. Impossible that a child, *her* child, was here with her.

They had hoped for more children but Katie never conceived again. Tempted to believe that new things couldn't be started in a place with a history as dark as this one, Zachariah grew strangely superstitious. He wondered if his greed to stretch his money further, or to exceed his father's living, hadn't brought him into a place where things much greater than money were at stake.

Much like the late August air following out the rain, the time passed away from him. Years went by, not in the form of years with their quartered shape, but in the form of seasons shaped more or less independently of one another, some lean and hard and others so perfect you felt the hand of God on everything. Zachariah owned an amount of land his father would never have dreamed of and he had managed to keep it even as others had lost everything.

In the last season of his life, one short Georgia winter in his sixty-eighth year, he woke and found he was unable to move his legs. He had been walking the day before, he had carried a wet harness that must have weighed ninety pounds. And now he could not wiggle his toes. It parted his mind like thunder and he wept. Soon his arms did not work. Soon he stared into his wife's eyes with longing, like a confession he could not make, an apology for bringing them down to Georgia. He could see those houses they passed that first day, see their dark shadows. Katie fed him and he could not speak to her. Within the week he died of polio.

Katie lived four more years. She lived in the same house with her son and his new wife and spent her last weeks in a bed in the new room her son had built for her. The room was added onto the house behind the kitchen and lined with fresh heart-pine paneling, cut tongue and groove, and smelled sweet like the slick floor of a cool pine stand in early spring. The room had three large windows that operated with little hand-cranks and could swing open. Thaddeus would come down in the mornings and open the windows as she slept. She often dreamed that the wall had been removed and that birds were resting on her nightstand and headboard. She had never in her life been so happy or felt so close to her son as when she slept in the room he made for her. Just outside the window was a good sized dogwood. In her last week she watched each day as the new green branches budded and leaved and she felt the tree's joy inside her, a slow unrelenting joy and she was overwhelmed with gratitude. She had a dream again that the wall was gone but this time the tree reached into the room and lifted her and held her like a small child. In the dream her tongue melted in her mouth and it tasted like corn pudding. She left the room that morning when the wall rolled up like a curtain. She felt her breathing pause, and then stop. She could not open her eyes but she could feel the breeze moving her hair. This is all real, she thought, and I am real, and I will continue to be real.

Thaddeus married Bethany when she was sixteen, he twenty-six. He brought her to live with his mother and spent some of his father's timber holdings on renovating the house. She was a healthy woman with curly brown hair and large, shallow-set eyes that were at times a light blue and at other times field green.

Despite her health, Bethany lost three of their four children in childbirth on account of what doctors called her "narrow passage." The first time the doctor used those words Thaddeus couldn't help but think of a picture he saw once. It was a finely detailed etching printed on an inserted page in the back of his father's Bible. In the picture was the image of a narrow gate through which golden rays shined. Standing beside the gate was a rich man who had a team of mules and an over-loaded wagon. In the back of the wagon were packages labeled "pride," "greed," "selfishness," and other sins that Thaddeus couldn't remember. What Thaddeus *could* remember was the mournful way the driver had his back bent and his face buried in his hands. Bethany Harden Shockley died at twenty-one while giving birth to their fourth and only surviving child, one she hoped to name after her father, James Warren.

After Bethany died Thaddeus was never able to completely distinguish himself from the image of the man left beside the bright gate. In his mind the gate went both ways, not one. His son James came into the world just as Bethany went out of it and so it was Thaddeus who had been left standing there beside the gate, or so it seemed, with his face buried in his hands.

Before James Warren Shockley had even learned his alphabet he knew how to pick a cotton shrub bare. Thaddeus put him to work early in part to suppress the boy's willfulness—which was apparent early on—and in part because Thaddeus just didn't know what else to do with a child. He was as hard on James as his father had been hard on him. One might have thought that James's increasing resemblance to his mother would have spared him some of his father's demands but it wasn't the case. Thaddeus confused his pain and shared it all, every ounce of it, with the boy.

Thaddeus had a stroke late one afternoon coaxing his mules into dragging a skid of cotton. He had a module on the skid behind the team and was working it slowly out to the road. He collapsed perfectly in between two furrows so that James couldn't see him from the house. James saw the team standing restless and unattended beneath their yoke and it was a long walk to where he found his father. Thaddeus was lying on his side, looking both frail and stiff, like something that would crumble if you kicked it. James was alone now, still a young man, and *alone*; he could never have imagined a world without his father, his father's relentless body and tirelessness and now he was suddenly alone in the world. He owned it all, everything.

The year Thaddeus died was the same year James spent his entire inheritance—a mortgage on the property and some money from the sale of the timber on the back of the lot, timber his father refused to harvest—on pecan saplings. James was only seventeen years old then, but he had learned everything there was to know about cotton including the fact that it would kill you before it made you any money.

He would manage hardwood trees instead, harvesting their timber holdings on a ten-year cycle, and he would plant pecans in the acreage around the house and the other cleared fields and that would be his living. He had always loved the shade of the big scarred pecan in the front of their house, the way it held the light of early spring, diffused it into a harmless pattern, the heavy fruit that brought the tall, gray deer at twilight in summer when other mast crops were scarce. It seemed right to turn the land into a grove, right in a way he couldn't name, as if the image of a grove had been implanted in his mind from a young age. He could see the turkeys wandering in groups now in the break-up of light beneath the heavy canopy, the light playing on their feathers in the distance like something divine crawling all over them; he could see all of this and it seemed the only way—the path of life for not only him but for a family that didn't exist yet.

His father's only real friend, a red-faced man named William Pritchard, gave the sermon at the funeral and also tossed in the first shovelful of dirt. After the funeral William told James there was talk of a new mill going up in Milledgeville. Shipping costs would be next to nothing. James said he didn't care if there were forty mills going up in Milledgeville. Then the saplings went in the ground and William understood.

One evening William made a visit, sat down on the front porch and told James that pecans took too long and were too temperamental to make good on. The next week the Depression came on strong in Sparta, as it did for all of Georgia, and the textile mill in Savannah went belly up just as the exterior walls were bricked in. It sat there as empty as a bombed-out factory, filling with kudzu and sunlight and nothing else.

In its prime—the summer of 1956—the pecan grove yielded seven hundred pounds per acre. James had his family in a good place. The house Zachariah and Katie had established was a small pine-paneled cabin, to which his father Thaddeus added rooms and a covered porch. But James turned the house into a two-story white-washed address, a fine house easily distinguished from the road. The pecan grove surrounded it entirely, taking up ten acres out front and thirty out back. In the back lot one tree stood taller than the others, over mature, its limbs heavy under their own girth, the bark darker and thicker, its plates and rifts deeper, with unexplainable scars high on its trunk. James left this tree standing though it was too old to produce a good crop. It had been his inspiration, and he thought it deserved to stand as long as it could.

James had other groves now, bought or leased in various places in the county, but the grove around his house was the first, the oldest, and by far the most majestic. The spacing was perfectly even between the trees and James made sure when he planted that the driveway was parallel to their lines so he wouldn't have to lose any trees on account of it. The effect of those vast and evenly-spaced pecans and the long shafts of light that fell between them gave visitors the feeling they were driving through the portico of some ancient temple, James Warren's house the altar. It was an impressive sight, more impressive still in the springtime when the leaves unfolded and formed a ceiling over the grove, a vibrant back-lit roof.

James Warren married Anne Elizabeth Pritchard when he was twenty-eight years old. She was William's oldest daughter, a seventeen-year-old girl with warm skin and long dark hair. She had eleven brothers and sisters and that was all James knew about her. One afternoon she was out with six of her brothers and two of her sisters. They were walking down the road with their cotton sacks full. He was coming home with a brand new hopper he had shipped into Milledgeville the day before. He told the boys to get in the back if they wanted a ride and he told the girls they could ride in the cab.

Anne sat against the door of the truck with one sister between them and the other in her lap. As the truck rose and fell in the smooth clay runnels, she fell asleep with her forehead against her little sister's neck. James noticed her hands, how one lay in a loose fist, the other turned over on her sister's leg. The tips of her fingers were raw and red from the bolls.

The sight of those hands put an ache in his heart. At night, as he turned in his bed, he couldn't see anything else but her and no amount of work tired him properly.

He had to go over the next week to set it up with her father. He paid William three hundred dollars to offset the work he was getting from the girl. The two were married four weeks later. In the first year they had a son named Silas Temperance Shockley. By then James Warren had gotten used to being in control of most things. He made a shaker out of an old Dodge Ram turned backward so that the engine was in the rear to counterweight the arm that would grab the tree trunk. He had even learned how to beat the rosette disease by putting zinc in his fertilizer. He shook trees all season, the fruit coming down like heavy rain against the hood of the Dodge, and prosperous, oh prosperous.

Silas

How rare the bird is I may not say being the only specimen I have ever seen.

—John James Audubon

H E WAS CAUGHT FIRST BY HIS MOTHER. Anne heard the sounds of bare footfall on the kitchen tiles late that evening and dressed herself in the hallway outside her bedroom, careful not to wake her husband. In the kitchen she found the screen door cracked open, a pair of jeans clumped in the yawn of the door. Stuffed down inside the jeans was a pair of her son's underpants. Outside, on the first two steps, lay a pair of dirty socks, and on the last a wadded T-shirt.

She turned off the light in the kitchen and then went into the living room. She looked out behind the house into the dim grove and saw nothing. The rows of pecan trees fell away and converged farther than her eyes could follow. At the front of the house she put her face to the window, cupping her hands against the cold glass, and for a moment saw nothing. And then, out by the road, outlined in the scant moonlight was her son, standing without a stitch of clothing on.

Anne watched as if spellbound, feeling a strange warmth move across her skin as the boy ran between the trees, reaching out his hand to touch the trunks, circling one after another.

She watched him until his motion, from tree to tree, took him out of her sight; it looked like some unworldly ritual, and it stirred her mind. Who are you? she thought.

That night she folded her son's clothing neatly and left it for him on the top step of the kitchen stairs, as if to say, "This won't sit well with your father."

A week later she woke in the middle of the night to find her husband standing by the bedroom window. His chest and arms blanched by the weak light that fell between the stiles.

"James?" she asked.

"Thought I heard something," he said.

She had hoped that the boy would go through this phase, this behavior, undetected. Or maybe she hoped her warning—an offering of folded clothes—would put an end to this before her husband found out.

"You were dreaming," she said, patting the sheets beside her.

"I wasn't," he said. "Now hush."

A long moment passed, and Anne filled it with the image she knew would soon appear, of Silas running barefoot in the season before the shake, when there was no husk of crop on the ground. James tilted his head to one side and moved his face even closer to the window. "What in God's name?" he said. He went to the foot chest and stepped into his pants and pulled on his shirt and was out the door before it was buttoned.

The boy was brought back into the house and examined in the kitchen before being given a chance to put his clothing back on. James wanted to quote a scripture to his son—a custom in their house before punishment of any kind—something about nudity or nighttime or both, but he could think of nothing that applied. Instead he looked hard at Silas and said, "Do you see any deer, cattle, or hogs living in this house with us?"

"No, sir," Silas said, following the logic with care.

"Do you want to go out to live with them?"

"No, sir," he said again.

"You'll keep your clothes on in and out of this house unless you're bathing. You understand?"

Silas's eyes crept up the arch of a long switch resting loosely in his father's right hand. There were slips of ripe green along its shaft where his father had shaved off the buds. For a reason he could not name, maybe nervousness or because he had no explanation, Silas began to smile. He felt the smile creep into the muscles of his face, a tightness, as if his face had been plunged into cold water, and he knew he couldn't keep the smile from arriving and that it was a horrible thing and that fact only made the smile determine itself. He was stark naked, standing in the dim kitchen, and now, to his horror, he was grinning at his father.

"This won't be funny," his father said. He put his large hand on the narrow shoulder and turned Silas against the refrigerator and brought the switch down on the fair thighs and legs, invoking dark purple welts on the skin.

Silas was more careful the next time. He performed his rite farther from the house, deeper in the avenues of the grove. He was caught a second time but only because James had gotten into the habit of wakening in the middle of the night and walking down the hall to the boy's room. That night, after finding his son's bed empty, James went out into the grove like a fury, calling the boy's name. It seemed for a while that Silas would remain in the cold, waiting out his father. James continued to call—assuring the boy that he would wait for him all night and all morning, for as long as Silas liked—and after several more minutes Silas appeared, again completely nude, summoned from the trees like a ghost. It was late November, and the breath from the two bodies, one clothed and one bare, one breathing heavily from exertion and the other from pain, poured out in thick clouds that hung around them and slowly dissipated. The switch went to work again on the boy's legs and back. This time it moved faster than before, fast enough to open the skin where it was most tender, behind the knees, across the lower back. It was the last time Silas went running in the grove undressed, and they never mentioned it again as a family.

James understood that night that his son was something he would never completely comprehend. There were, of course, some things in the boy that reminded James of himself, his willfulness especially. But there was another side, he realized, a hemisphere waxed always away from him, the tidal lock of an unlit landscape he couldn't map or reckon with.

Silas found ways to remain true to all of James's suspicions. He was largely indefinable. He didn't make friends easily, or at all, and regardless of how much work James put on him he still read too many books and developed one too many odd habits. He ate his plate clockwise, in spite of which vegetables were his favorites; he would fill the sink in his bathroom with water and hold his hands beneath and stare at them for hours; he liked to lie in small spaces for long periods of time, being denied his dinner on multiple occasions to spend the entire evening beneath the rolltop desk in the living room. Even his mother was unnerved when he started keeping cicada molts in his bedroom like pets, long trains of them clinging to the window curtains.

At the age of thirteen Silas started sleeping in his closet. He made a pallet on the floor out of towels and would sleep there with the door closed. After noticing the bed was often immaculately made and that many of her towels were missing, Anne finally discovered his nest. She folded the towels and clothing neatly and put them away. The next day the nest was back, and then, a few months later, it was abandoned and the bed again showed signs of use.

At sixteen Silas suddenly decided that he didn't want to have anything to do with pecan farming or Sparta. Without warning he told his father that he wanted to go to college in Milledgeville, or Atlanta, even. They were riding out to another grove with the hopper in tow. Long ribbons of dust unspooled behind the truck in both directions, and Silas watched them despondently in his side-view mirror, and then he spoke, casually, as if he were commenting on the weather. James pulled the truck to the side of the road and glared at the boy. He told him that pecans and Sparta had everything to do with him and that he would do good to start getting his mind around that fact. He would be fourth to run the place.

"There was Zachariah," his father said, counting his heavy fingers like gravestones, "then Thaddeus, then me, and then there's you. Most people work their whole lives to get what you already got. You got a people and place that's yours and no one else's, so don't ever speak that way again."

Silas knew everything there was to know about pecans. He knew how to repair the hopper and even built a new hopper that ran smoother than the old catalog ones. He knew, simply by holding the firstfruits of the October shake, how the rain had affected the yield for that year. It seemed that pecans were all he was supposed to know about the world, and the knowledge left him often with a powerful curiosity and at other times a desperate feeling, as if he were tethered to something very dense and small and unaffected.

Later that same year Silas found that he had a particular talent. It came to him so naturally it was as if he had walked backward into it. He could carve blocks of wood into miniature birds. The first bird he carved was a mallard, and he carved it in woodshop class for an assignment. The week before, they had made wooden toolboxes, and Silas found the project tedious, the template traced out, the dowel rod run through. He finished his toolbox quickly and sat at his desk sanding it down, making the edges of his box beveled and smooth like flour on a countertop.

The bird project was different. It required an ability to see forms and contours where there were none, to take something rigid and ordinary and to find in it something lifelike and faithful. The mallard he carved that afternoon in class was nothing manifold, remarkable only in its proportion and shape. There were no feathers but two very shapely wings and a long tail. The head, especially, was exactly like that of a duck. The woodshop teacher held the bird in his hand and said, "Silas, now that's really something." And Silas agreed. It was something, or it meant something. He took the bird home and buried it in the soft sand beneath the back porch and went inside and washed up for dinner.

Silas's grandfather Thaddeus had left a good set of gouges and chip knives in the lean-to shed behind the new barn. The shed had long before been turned into storage and held all sorts of relics hidden among the piles of scrap. The tools were beautiful, sopped with oil and marked with his grandfather's initials. The chip knives were wrapped in a soft leather pouch along with some narrow rasps and files, and there were pockets for each tool. Tied with a leather strap across the bottom was a whetstone and a small punch. From out behind the shed Silas dragged in an old galvanized bathtub, which he turned over to use as his workbench.

At the library he found a field guide to North American birds, and before he was home he set his mind to the task of reproducing each one. There was plenty of pecan for stock, and though the wood was harder than he would have liked, its color and grain were pleasing. Silas found that he could reproduce the bird's proportions easily, as if by instinct, and he also found that if he was careful enough, if he traced the feather designs out in pencil, he could reproduce them in great detail. He would trace a shape onto the square block, a line of motion meaningless to anyone but himself, and then start into his curves with a small draw knife, cutting always toward that invisible form, listening to the almost inaudible rustle of instinct, when to stop, when to turn. Once a bird was complete Silas would bury it beneath the porch with the others. When there was no more room beneath the porch, he buried it out in the grove.

His father was slow to notice the little mounds of raised dirt appearing in the coppice. At first he believed them the work of a mole, and then a whole family of moles. When the patches continued to appear, scattered throughout the grove over the course of a few months, he decided to deal with it. One morning while Silas was in school, he took a shovel to investigate the freshly turned earth. In less than a minute James found himself holding what looked to be a small wooden blue jay. It was wet, its grain darkened from the soil. He didn't for a moment believe that Silas had made the bird, but he was certain that Silas alone was somehow involved in its burial. What now? he thought.

He walked around the grove for half an hour finding other

birds, each buried at the same swift depth. Two looked the same as the first. They were birds with a steeply crowned head, like a cardinal or a jay. And then there was one not yet finished, its form half-cast into the block so that it seemed to be some kind of study for the others. James stared at it in perplexity.

The sight of the bird's finely jointed legs, one leg out of the block completely, the other just on the brink of emerging, was at once miraculous and eerie. It was as if the bird were alive and trying to free itself from the wood. It stirred his heart and filled him with a longing to understand. He held it up close to his face, as if it were a great question, an impossible sign.

He scrambled in the yard to turn up each bird, leaving the shovel behind in fear that he would damage them. He panicked at the soil with his bare hands. Once a bird was upturned he would stare at it for a long time before placing it in a pocket he had formed out of the front of his shirt.

The last bird he upturned wasn't the last he might have found, but it was all he could stand. It was a common woodcock, but nothing about the carving was common. The woodcock had been captured in the motion of preening its feathers. Its head was turned down to the side, its beak extending out over a wing raised away from its breast. The feathers were incredible in their detail, fanned away from the breast, each layered carefully on top of the other. This happened to be the most recent bird Silas had carved, and it represented a new development in his skill—the representation of motion.

James carried these birds inside his untucked shirt to the kitchen table. He laid them down and wiped the remaining dirt off them with his hands. He lined them up on the tablecloth and sat down before them in a stupor, as if they would soon begin to speak, as if he should be ready for such a thing to occur.

Anne found her husband sitting across from the birds, his hand over his mouth, his shirt covered in dirt. He looked up at her, let his hand drop from his face, and opened his mouth to speak but said nothing.

"Where did these come from?" Anne asked, though she knew well enough and wasn't certain what her husband would do or think.

"Silas did 'em," he said. "I think he did every one of 'em."

Anne then led her husband outside to the old lean-to shed. James hadn't set foot in his father's storage shed for months now. Out past the end of his wife's extended finger was the overturned washtub covered with curly locks of wood. Atop the tub lay a bird in process. A small bird, the struggle of appearance still evident in its pose. Beside it was one of Thaddeus's gouges. James sat down heavily on the bucket his son used as a chair. He picked up his father's gouge and studied it, then put it back down. He gathered a handful of wood shavings and let them drop between his feet.

"You ever seen anything like it?" he asked his wife.

She shook her head and turned back inside, leaving him sitting there on the bucket like a man who had been knocked down in a fight.

James had intended to spend that afternoon taking samples from each acre to check for rosette disease in the crop. Instead, he found himself suddenly thrown into a series of new errands, and he moved with earnestness, one task begetting another—as action creates a taste for itself—until his engagements overtook his mind.

He backed his truck up to the shed. He dragged the washtub out and cleared the floor and the space beneath the shelves of every odd thing his father and grandfather had kept out of suspicion of future use. Pieces of rusted rake implements, soiled stacks of almanacs and catalogs, the detritus of a chain saw that never ran, a wheelbarrow axle, and many other hopeless, handed-down things were thrown into the back of his truck to be hauled to the dump. He removed all his father's scrap hardware from the sagging shelves, swept them clean of dust, then reset them with fresh joists and angles. When the shed was clear he built a low worktable against the back wall—two sawhorses and two heavy planks, recently milled, that he'd intended to sell, beautiful and gray in their patina, flat as calm water. He took his wife's stool from the kitchen and placed it under the table, knowing he would have to buy her another one. Beneath the wall on the far side he dug a hole and ran an extension cord and hung a bare bulb for a work light, testing it several times. He found a kerosene heater, which he cleaned and refilled and lit, and it filled the room with its warm tang. Time seemed to press on his heart, and he looked constantly at his watch, hurrying to complete the intention he himself barely understood. It was nearly three when he rehung the doors so they would close soundly and retain the heat.

When he was finished he stood for a long time in the door frame and surveyed his labor. The carved birds were now lined across the shelves above the bench, wet with linseed and tung oil, their grain alive in the light. He brought his wife to see, and she stood for a long time looking at the shelves. It seemed as if an entire flock of exiles had roosted there and made for themselves an aviary that stood sentient over the artist's vise and table.

After some time James left the shed and went into the house and took a shower, his thoughts left unuttered, his hands still wishing for something more to do, to add to the place he had made.

That night Silas never came into the house. Anne and James ate dinner together in perfect silence, their son's plate untouched at the end of the table. They went to bed, and still, late into the night, the light in the shed made long chinks in the dark.

An olive-sided flycatcher swept across the panels, casting bolts of shadow; a Blackburnian warbler rested over the table and sang something previous and inscrutable. The light burned on—the hybridists in their beds, their young at his work—and mimicked that greater light inside the mother and father. Anne turned into her husband's back and slept and James lay drifting off, listening to some dream of crank flight, the whistle of wings as the covey rose and dispersed into the limbs of the grove.

Lipochrome

God will give you blood to drink.
—Sarah Good

IT DID NOT GO AWAY—AS EVERYONE said it would. At nine months Lorrie was diagnosed with an obscure disorder thought to be caused by an infection in the eyes at birth, a condition that amplifies the production of rare pigments in the iris, increasing them until they dominate the eye. When most baby's eyes shift from the lapis slate of infancy to their final and common color, Lorrie's eyes turned wolf yellow. They smoldered under her white bonnet like filaments at low voltage.

This was startling to everyone. To her parents. To those who cooed and drew close to see her. To those who lifted her cap to peer in at the bland, lost little face. And there everyone found those lupine eyes, gold rivets. Soon people lost their inhibitions completely. "Can I see?" they asked, waving and jogging toward her across the square that divided the cemetery from the churchyard, following the poor mother into stores, down the produce aisle. Often that first year Lorrie's mother would turn to find a strange man standing behind her, cornering her against the lettuce. No introductions. "Mind if I have a look?"

And what could she do? She would turn her child from her shoulder, bob her on her forearm and let the stranger stare into Lorrie's eyes. "Ain't that a thing," some said. "They'll go away," said others.

What happened when she was fourteen was in many ways inevitable. She had been so long an object of curiosity—a kind of unconsummated desire—and the rumors had been in composition from the very beginning, waiting for their turn in the wings, jealous and impatient like understudies: "I bet she has a forked tongue." "I bet she howls at night."

After church that morning her mother stayed and talked while Lorrie wandered outside to wait on the warm steps. From there she saw a horse standing across the street in the shade of a tremendous live oak. It was tied by the bosal to an ornamental iron fence capped with sharp hand-hammered finials. The fence had been there for a hundred years and it lifted and sunk where the roots of the oak pressed up beneath it, causing sections of finials to aim inward in concave depressions and others to fan out lethally like the rays of the sun on old celestial maps.

She was moved toward the horse by a restless feeling the church service put inside her. Like the residue a flash bulb leaves hanging in the air—an exposure that turns with you when you turn and stays out in front of you when you close your eyes—the long stillness of the hour had made the world distant and unreal and the horse was a part of the dream. She wanted to touch the tight tendons of the leg, wanted to run her hand over the muscles and across the steep hill of the flank.

As her hand neared the front shoulder it seemed a spark

left her fingertips, and if not a spark, something like it, something inside her, something she carried that leapt. An invisible surface was breached. The animal spooked and reared and she fell back and watched as the horse grew tall and then taller again, impossibly tall. It came down near her, the hooves clattering on stone. A taste of iron in her mouth, a notch in the tip of her tongue, a smell like fear. The horse went up again and she watched as it tried to clear the old iron fence. She watched as the mecate caught and the historic finials disappeared into the smooth barrel of the horse's underbelly.

The sound it made was significant, married to its meaning. A song somewhere inside the sound drew men toward it. From the far end of the road, and from around the corner, and from across the street, they hustled toward the sound of the horse, animal in hysteric pain. But the noise Lorrie heard had not come from the horse but from somewhere inside her. The sound was the sound of her mind when she saw the horse descend, it was the sound of a sawmill clutch before the belt gains, the sound of resistance, of wishing it could all be turned back, the sound of a loud blister in her palm after a day of raking leaves, the long wooden pews creaking, the organ growl, the doxology, pedal tones that are felt before they can be heard. It was a sound like the nameless world.

The horse's front hooves pawed and reached for the ground while the animal remained suspended. On the sidewalk, in the shadow, it seemed the horse was running hard in a four-beat gait and the shadow was something projected out of the horse, some vital extension escaping.

The mare bled out from its barrel. Sun warmed berries. The eye, much larger than her own, widened above her. She watched the eye as the blood left the horse, black ink streaming down

the scrollwork, over the nodes and twisted pickets. The big eye
rolled languidly and then centered itself like the bi-point globe
inside her father's liquid compass, regaining its mysterious traction to the world. She watched the eye work to stay in the world,
to keep a hold on it.

Men seemed to come from everywhere then. They mobbed
around her, hurt by excitement, shouting to each other, crowding in. Their boot heels slipped in the blood, streaking it with
clay. They scurried around the horse's suspended body, over
the fence, placing their backs alongside the animal's body
and lifting with their legs. This was all organized by shouting
and by something unspoken, the frantic purposeful feeling,
not unlike joy, a joy men take in things terrible and unlikely.
Shouts rose suddenly to stop lifting; a man who did not hear
fell to the ground beneath the horse and when he rose his dark
suit pants were purple with blood and brilliant in the sunlight.
The mare squealed when the lifting stopped and stamped its
back legs and the men around it moved away and the horse
descended only farther into the finials until it stood with its
front hooves on the ground. It rested. It contemplated its pain.

Everyone on that corner knew it was Quatrous's horse and
that he had just bought it the week before. He was one of the
only men in Shell Bluff to still bring a horse into town and it
was only on Sundays. Quatrous made the decision. He stepped
out of the church across the street and without looking twice
at the scene—the men sweating, their feet slipping in the
blood—he asked one of the police officers for a pistol.

Lorrie had been carried across the street and propped up
against the trunk of a large sweet gum tree. Her eyes were
glazed and the world inside her pitched and turned. Her
mother took off her shoes and threw them away and held

her face and stared into it and saw nothing but the vivid gold eyes, focusing on nothing. The pistol snapped, ringing the air between the short buildings, and the horse sunk entirely into the finials as a large flock of pigeons rushed out from the limbs above Lorrie's head.

The women in the prayer meetings shuddered to hear each new story—though they, most of all, spread them around— and would then commence to praying for Lorrie and her freedom from what they called her *oppression*. Many believed the incident to be associated somehow with her grandmother's wedding band and wished Lorrie to take the band off.

Lorrie's grandmother had lived with them for as long as Lorrie could remember and her presence in their house was robust, solid, heavy with laughter. Her grandmother seemed so physical an object, and by comparison her parents, who were not affectionate people, seemed frail, as if strong laughter would sift them right out of the world like ash.

Lorrie would sit with the old woman in the evenings for hours and run her fingers down the large distended blue veins in her hands, tracing them as they warped over the bones, pressing them down and watching them grow faint, disappear, and then appear again. Her grandmother never resisted being touched and Lorrie loved this about her. She would let Lorrie do her hair up in all sorts of bizarre arrangements, twists and bows with confectionary zeal, everything short of cutting it, and the grandmother sat with her eyes closed, drifting in and out of sleep.

Lorrie was twelve when her grandmother died and her grief was immense. The wedding band was left to her for her own wedding day, but she refused to leave it in its envelope in the stationery desk. She screamed when it was asked of her and the screaming rattled her mother's nerves. She was allowed to wear the ring, with the exception that she was only allowed to wear it on her right hand. It fit loosely on her slim fingers and Lorrie developed the habit of keeping that hand pursed into a fist when she walked or ran, giving her appearance a new ferocity, as if she were perpetually charging up to sock someone in the mouth.

After the horse died a series of stories developed. Desire was let free. One of the first stories that circulated throughout Shell Bluff—and even beyond, into Milledgeville and Sparta—was one that a number of people attested to seeing personally. Her grandmother's wedding band would disappear from Lorrie's finger and reappear in her throat. It happened at school. The ring appeared suddenly in her throat and was trying to choke her. Miss Addison slapped her firmly on the back and out fell her grandmother's ring onto the floor.

"Why'd you swalla that?" the teacher asked.

"She didn't though," said another girl. "It disappeared right off her finger. I saw the whole thing. It was there and then it was in her throat and she was choking. It showed up in her throat. I saw it all. I saw the lump in her throat. It's trying to kill her."

The word "booger" and the song "Lorrie and her booger sitting in a tree. . ." became a musical phrase that lived in Lorrie's landscape, a bobwhite's call, a whippoorwill. The sounds of the words and the notes of the song were factual things that traveled through the air and scared her. She was oppressed. She was prayed for. All of it scared her.

Soon Lorrie hated being left alone, certain now, after all the words, and songs, and tauntings, and prayers, that when she was alone she was not. Her fear of being alone, the fear itself, fed the rumors and as the rumors grew so did her reluctance to be around too many people, or too few people, or to come near an animal, any animal, which could be difficult when almost everyone in Shell Bluff owned some amount of livestock.

There were other things to reignite the story whenever it seemed to be wavering: a girl said she had a secret to tell. Her name was Mccuen. She had six brothers all called by the same last name and no one knew their first names. They were Mccuens. To call one was to call them all, but for Lorrie, Mccuen was the girl who reeked of kerosene during the short Georgia winters. She was the girl who lived with her tribe of brothers and was skinned-kneed and ugly in appearance despite the fine features of her face and the way the eyelids lay softy over the almond-shaped eyes, as if they were perpetually half-closed.

Mccuen led Lorrie by the hand into the bathroom stall and instead of disclosing a secret began to softly stroke her arms, and then her cheeks and hair. Lorrie felt the pressure of the girl's hand on her head and then the hand moved to her cheek and then to her shoulder and Lorrie's heart began to pound and at the same time she struggled to keep her eyes open, as if she were running full speed into sleep.

After the first kiss Lorrie let her lips part and Mccuen kissed her again and it summed in her mind into a litany. It was a hot afternoon along a bank of red maples turning suddenly cool; it was water dripping off her fingertips, tugging each finger toward the ground with invisible force; it was her hand swollen from a wasp sting, a hand that was numb and large and didn't feel like her own when she touched it with the other; it was six pieces of coal she once found in her school desk, black like sin; it was soft like owl feathers and heavy like fruit.

They might have kissed a thousand times—it seemed an infinite space between each one. She never kissed back but it did not matter, she did not have to. They came one after the other. There was another girl there who saw them standing together, who had walked in quietly behind them and saw their shoes staggered in, facing each other. And she could tell, she just could, by the position of their feet and the odd silence, and she knew what was happening. It was this girl, hurt with longing and self-consciousness, who told her mother what she had not seen but knew, who told her friends that she had seen what she had not, who told everyone she could that Lorrie had seduced Mccuen with her witch eyes. She added to the story as it needed it, added that she heard them speaking together, in one voice speaking, and that they spoke in a language she had never heard before.

Lorrie's parents received visitors who offered their advice, who spoke of how they had cured their own children from similar dispositions. Mccuen spent two weeks out of school and no one knew what happened to her those two weeks, but when she returned to school she never looked at Lorrie again.

A few months passed and Lorrie was exhausted and numb to everything. She avoided animals completely, certain that whatever was with her would scare them, cause them to jump off of cliffs, or so she was told, or hurl themselves onto sharp objects.

Lorrie would be made a member of the church by Quatrous in early August. She completed her confirmation class uneventfully and the date was printed in the church bulletin with the names of the other children to be made members. The following week Lorrie's name stood alone and the other baptisms were all rescheduled.

On the afternoon of the event Lorrie was picked up along with her family by a tall young man with greasy hair who drove a long pink Buick convertible. He introduced himself as James. James had just come down from Columbia with his new wife and was excited to be a part of the occasion. On hearing from his brother-in-law that there would be a baptism he insisted on driving the family. He treated them like prominent figures in a grand parade. He left the top down on the Buick. He spoke loudly, over the radio—which he did not turn down, even as he pulled into the church parking lot to meet the caravan that contained the minister and what seemed a large number of cars and trucks that would follow them to the river. Compared to her father's truck, the Buick went smoothly along Landing Road, suggesting the familiar road with its washed-out creeks and roots but transcending it. Soon the other cars in their party were not visible. Lorrie gave up tucking her hair behind her ears and let it swirl around her face while her mother kept both her hands on her hat and her father wore his dark suit and a tight smile across his embarrassed face.

"I remember my first baptism," James yelled at his passengers. "I thought the man wouldn't ever let me up and when I did get up I tried to sock him in the face. He was messing with me. I swore he was. He looked small to me and I thought I could take him but he was strong as an ox. God. He was strong. He threw me right down again into the water and held me there until I gave up." He reached back and slapped Lorrie on the leg and laughed as the Buick veered slowly toward the tree line. He corrected into the road and aimed the rearview mirror at her. "So don't try it." He winked.

"I thought you said you didn't baptize till you married Q's little sister," Lorrie yelled back.

"Honey, that's not your place," her father turned.

"I didn't," James said.

"But you were baptized as a little boy?" she asked.

"Honey," her father said again.

"That's true," he declared, laughing, "I got baptized as a boy but didn't get saved till I married Q's sister. I guess I was on layaway."

James's laughter caused the limbs to shake overhead and the light to spill down through the trees. He had tears in his eyes he was laughing so hard and the car was swerving and Lorrie felt herself being made new. Thurston Harris's *Litty Bitty* was playing on the radio and the music was infecting them all, a strange sense of buoyancy entered her bones, she would walk across the water, she would bob like a cork. They smiled as they looked at each other, a family but strangers to themselves, figures made from air and sugar and gossamer, confections from a dream.

Baptisms were carried out in an eddy along the Savannah River where it takes Miller's Pond Creek. There was a sandy wash a few steps up the creek mouth with good shallow clear water and the current was soft. Quatrous often said he loved the spot. It reminded him of those lesser-known lines from Cloverdale. "Lead me forth beside the waters of comfort."

"You see, the water doesn't need to be still," he would say on a Sunday morning, "'cause the best water keeps on moving, don't it. You go get a drink from Telfair Pond up above the dam and tell me it don't taste a slick froggy. Now go get you a drink from Keysville at the head and you'll lay yourself face down and say Lord have mercy. Good water knows it's not done. It's got a race to run along the earth. Amen? It's not home. No. But it's bringing home with it, just not there yet. Who else ain't home? We aren't. That's right."

As the cars pulled up they could already see it wouldn't do. The river was swollen and banking violently. The party walked the upstream path together in a single file just to see how the creek mouth looked and it didn't look any better. What had once been an eddy was a brown, churning place. Every so often a log would drift in and spin a few times like it was in a washer and then shoot back out into the river.

The men stood on the bank watching the river surge by, already intoxicated by the level sheen of light—if only it were small enough for them to run their hand across it, like a table top, to examine it, they would. Quatrous took off his shoes and rolled up his pant legs and prepared to wade in a few feet where it seemed the slowest. He needed to see how bad it actually was before he would give up his spot.

"Easy now," James said, laughing.

"Woooo," Quatrous said to the crowd, widening his eyes. They laughed.

"Is it cold enough?" James yelled.

"Woooo," he said again, "no, it's tugging though. It's tugging."

He waded back carefully and reached his hand up to James to help him step out just as he slipped in the slick kaolin clay that banded the bank. He went down on his face before he could get his hand down and the current pulled him immediately out of the creek mouth and as it did he rolled casually onto his back as if he were expecting as much to happen. It seemed like his belly was made of cork the way he shot out into the Savannah, bobbing in the rapids as he accelerated. He was cruising very quickly out of sight, disappearing in the shade of large maples and hickories and then reappearing on the other side moving faster than he was before and then he was gone.

Lorrie and James were racing along the bank shouting with others, James running ahead and laughing so hard he could barely keep Quatrous in sight. Lorrie's feet slapped along the packed footpath. She caught glimpses of Quatrous, down low close to the bank. He would occasionally roll onto his stomach and reach for a branch overhead and then, having missed it, roll onto his back to look where he was heading. When there wasn't a limb to reach for he kept his arms down by his side and used them as paddles to direct himself.

After two or three attempts he finally got hold of a low hanging possumhaw limb and was immediately stretched out longways downstream so that he couldn't get his feet underneath him to walk out for fear of increasing the drag and breaking the branch. They all moved to go down when James grabbed Lorrie by the arm and said, "No sugar, you stand right here." He made her hold on to a skinny tree and nodded to confirm that she would not leave it. He and another man went down the steep bank carefully together holding on to washed-out sycamore roots.

"You finished bathing?" he yelled down to Quatrous.

"I'm just thinking," Quatrous said.

"About how to get out?"

"No. About what it means."

"It means you're a clumsy old man, is what it means."

"Maybe. Maybe," he said, the water streaming around his face, framing his red skin. His thin white hair pasted and pulsing on his brow like a jellyfish.

"Do you want to hear my plan?" James said.

"Go ahead then."

"I'm gonna hold on to this tree with one hand and put the other on your arm and when you stand up the current is going to swing us around and pull you in to the bank and then you can grab those roots over there. How's that sound?"

"Sounds like a plan."

The rest of the party arrived as Quatrous was crawling carefully up the bank on his hands and knees and James was making his way up alongside, holding onto the trunks of trees, practically climbing from one to another. Lorrie's father held Quatrous under the arm as he stood. The preacher took off his tie and wrung it out. "Well, where to?" he said. "We might as well do this while I'm still wet."

Lorrie was baptized in a pond off Claxton-Lively Road. It was fed by an aquifer and it was the coldest water she could ever remember being in. He put her under and the water ran across her chest and she thought she felt her heart stop and it was hard to breathe. She was shivering so hard she couldn't walk. Quatrous lifted her up and carried her out of the pond and she sat down in the hot sand beside it while waves of dizziness, something near ecstasy, shot through her mind and body. The sun warmed her and she thought of nothing and it was in the nothing that the figures and voices of her life swung around her like a globe of stars being cranked and she heard the sound of the Buick's radio and she felt the heavy light entering her again, an opening in her mind, the opening of a fist.

It had been a little over a year since the horse had died and Quatrous thought it was time to bring her near an animal again. He thought they might give it a few tries, thought he would even teach her to ride and that the sight of her up on a horse would be good for the neighbors to see.

The Latvian was a heavier animal, good for light draft work and riding and, above all, calm as a tortoise. Lorrie was already standing when she saw Quatrous walking the animal around the bend in the road. Her dress was clenched in a ball in one fist above her knee, her other hand on the doorknob. Her eyes were wide and tracked the horse fiercely as they came. She stood like a deer at the edge of heavy woods, every nerve balanced. As soon as Quatrous turned up their long drive and it became clear he meant to visit the house she ducked inside.

He knocked on the door.

"Lorrie, come out here and meet this lady, she's real sweet."

He waited. He heard the mother and daughter talking softly.

"You want to know her name? Abigail. That's sweet, isn't?"

"Go on," her mother said.

Quatrous left the door and went down to the animal and petted it and pulled an apple from his pocket and fed it a bite and pulled the apple back.

"Want to feed her this apple?" he called.

Lorrie came out with an uncertain look on her face and took the apple carefully, keeping her eyes on the horse like it was a blasting cap.

"Go on," Quatrous said. He motioned with his hand how to lift the apple up. She watched the motion from the corner of her eye and lifted her hand up.

The horse took a step forward, moving her mouth out toward the apple. Lorrie pulled the apple back quickly and then launched it across the yard into the garden. The horse turned to watch the apple fly and when it turned back to her she caught it on the side of its nose with her closed fist. The Latvian's eyes grew wide. She slapped it several more times with her palm as it turned from her in a trot. She screamed and caught it once more on the flank with the flat of her hand, sending it into a steady gait out of the yard toward the road. A truck coming down the lane slammed on its brakes to let it pass. The horse swerved tight around the truck's hood, almost colliding with the fender before heading off in the opposite direction along the creek bed. It looked as if it would run the rest of the way home if home wasn't in the opposite direction. The mother screamed after her daughter but Lorrie did not stop. She disappeared after the horse, its newly long legs pawing the ground with incredible speed. "I'll grab the truck," the mother said. She went quickly inside the house. The screen door slammed.

Quatrous walked calmly out of the yard with his hands stuffed down in his pockets. His head down.

"Damn it," he said to himself.

As he came to the road he saw the hoofprints where they turned up the packed earth and he saw the ring lying brightly beside the spot in a slick of mud. He put his boot heel on top of it and pressed it down deep as if it were the head of snake. He kicked some earth over the spot to trod it down a second time and waited there for the mother.

The Firelighter

HE'D BEEN ACROSS THE RIVER ONCE BEFORE. That was down in Heloise with his father. They'd crossed on a ferry said to be the last place Jesse James was seen in public.

Hugh imagined the outlaw on that cold morning, saw him leaning impatiently on the port railing, shaking hands with strangers, smoking a cigar in a close-tailored sack suit.

"That was the last time he saw the river, then," Hugh noted sadly.

"He was mean," his father said. "Murdered and scalped unarmed civilians in Centralia with Bill Anderson." He grabbed Hugh under his chin, drug a pointer finger around the crown of his small head like a blade. "Cherokee blood, like you. His blade would start to itch." He tugged once on Hugh's hair and smiled, his eyes deep and gleeful. "You get that itch in your blood there's no getting it out."

The boy's mind raced. His scalp peeled away and the cold wind swirled up from the water to touch his wet skull. It would be so cold at first, and then it would burn, he thought, your skull laid bare to the world.

———

He was high above the water this time, crossing on the new Caruthersville bridge in his brother-in-law's shiny black car. His father was no longer alive and Hugh had forgotten about his Cherokee blood, forgotten that his great-grand-mother was chief Pathkiller's only daughter. For now he knew only that his sister was all he had in the world, and she was leaving.

He was going to live with his grandparents. Though they lived only in Steele, a few miles from Dyersburg on the Missouri side of the Mississippi, he had never met them. He did not want to live with them but his father had died and his sister was getting married and he had nowhere else to go.

The river swarmed beneath the bridge, muddy and pow-erful in the spring melt. He listened to the seams in the road-bed moan rhythmically under the tires. The tall bridge seemed to ignore the river, innocent of it like a bird. In the distance, a long barge drifted downstream, masses of pitch-soaked rail-road ties piled high on its back. He'd like to be on that barge, he thought, drifting slowly, close to the water.

Their names were Isaiah and Della Fairhart. He greeted them the way his sister taught him to greet adults, his chin up, hand ready to be shaken. With his chin raised he noticed how strongly he resembled the old man. Long arms, big hands, lank shoulders, the dark skin and broad nose. And the bones around the old man's eyes gathered like his own. He marveled at that. He had never seen his own resemblance in another person beyond his sister, but here his image emerged stronger than it had in his own father, a generation skipping once like a stone on glassy water.

"Happy birthday, Hugh," the old man said, "do you know how old you are?"

He did not realize it was his birthday. He had forgotten.

When he lived with his sister a man from the Tennessee custody courts came to visit twice a year and asked him each time how old he was and so he came into the habit of keeping the date in mind and always knowing the answer.

"Ten," Hugh said.

"You are indeed," the old man said.

Della, whom he would soon call Dell, gave him a paper bag with his name sewn on it in blue thread. The bag was full of oranges, hard candies, and a bar of chocolate. He kept the bag tucked under his arm even after he had taken a seat on his bed in a tremendous upstairs bedroom.

There were so many windows. When he lived with his sister they had only the one small window beside the front door. The back of their house was dug into the hill like the other houses nearby in Tennessee, framed with heavy timbers that smelled of sweet lamp oil. Now he had two windows of his own on adjacent walls. He went from one to the other many times, keeping the paper sack under his arm, feeling the shape of the oranges through the waxy paper.

The world outside wavered when he moved his eyes across the panes. He watched the draft animals moving down the road below the house. In the yard by the fence Della had planted large patches of white loosestrife that bloomed in tall goosenecks. In the breeze the flowers looked about nervously, like a flock. He wished his sister would have stayed with him; he wished he could show her the flowers and the candy and the many windows.

——

His grandfather died in 1936, two years after his sister married. Della died four years following and for the second time in his life, at the age of sixteen, he had lost his caretakers.

He missed his grandparents more than he could recall missing his father. He had spent his time with them learning how to live their life, how to split the white oak and black maple into fine stove-length pieces, how to take long walks in silence, following them down to a creek bed at the end of their road. Della liked to slip off her shoes and wade into the water, her dress splayed across the surface of the creek like the mouth of a foxglove blossom. Hugh and Isaiah would leave her there and walk along the creek until it divided into several springs that ran beneath the roots of large cedar trees, ducking under stones and roots as if the water were trying to return again, to find some hidden source.

The Cherokee in his blood, his grandfather used to say, would cause him to love the world if he would listen to it. "Pathkiller will come to you like the holy ghost," his grandfather told him "and fall on you and give you his spirit." In this way the holy ghost never took the form of a dove in Hugh's mind but instead a man who haunted all the paths of the world, a man who sprung from shady thickets of rhododendron, tomahawk raised, strange tongues of praise rising from his lips.

It never occurred to Hugh that he would not continue on in this rhythm for the rest of his life. He was too young to inherit anything directly from Della when she died. His sister was given the title to the house and William the power of attorney. But William would not accept guardianship of Hugh, saying Hugh was too old, and they sent him the papers he needed to sign for self-emancipation. In a letter his sister encouraged him to find work in Memphis.

A month had passed and he was still living in the house as if nothing had changed, except now he woke to cold rooms and lit the morning fires in the kitchen stove and no one woke him on Sundays for church. He would often fall asleep in the mornings on the sofa beneath a pile of blankets, forgetting to eat, not minding the chores, listening out for Della's soft footsteps, her steady movements still ghosting in the edge of his vision as the inchoate light rose and filled each room.

His sister's husband William sold the Fairhart house in Steele and invested the money in timber rights south of Bristol along Steel Creek. A new war loomed darkly that year and work turned up slowly to meet it.

Hugh started that year in a boarding house in Memphis, training during the day with the Illinois Central Railroad. In the city everyone was busy selling themselves to the war or preparing to, learning to fit themselves to a certain kind of work. He had to find a line, an entry point, a way to sell himself to the city. The war had resurfaced in Europe but had made the American railroad a powerful industry. All sorts of goods were moving east, huge stockyards full of cotton, minerals, all shipping across the Atlantic.

The railroad paid him for the training, the same rate as his working pay, and he took it home every night in a kind of amazement. Work for Isaiah and Della had never transformed into anything as abstract as money. This was a new and powerful feeling, the options limitlessness, he could turn money into anything.

The training lasted three working days and involved Hugh and four other boys standing on a train engine that wasn't running while an engineer shouted instructions from a platform and drank cold coffee from a silver whiskey flask. Hugh was to scoop the coal from the tinder bunker into the grate when the machine stoker failed. They practiced this, but there was no coal to scoop. He would get sand from a bag on the floor of his station when the sand line failed, and toss it under the driving wheels on both sides. They practiced this, too, but there was no sand. They flung their empty hands down on the motionless drive. He was to throw the snifting valve to let her coast, watch the rear bogie on turns, listen out for the coupling rods, oil this and that. The tall long-beaked oil cans sat nicely on a ledge over the grate opening, which kept the oil warm and slick. "Light and often," said the training engineer, "light and often. And don't leave holes on the fire bed, but don't pile it up neither. It'll smoke you out if it piles up."

The training engineer shouted and pointed and moved on before the boys knew exactly what they were supposed to be looking at. Three days like this, each boy holding a solid half-dollar in their pocket while nodding in mute incomprehension. They had minds all day only for what they could buy with that half-dollar, so heavy and cold it made them restless. They all thought about the same things, nothing being saved, the Coca-Cola and the cheeseburger they could get for fifteen cents, the movies they could watch for ten. Marlene Dietrich in *Destry Rides Again*: the beautiful woman in an illustrated poster six feet tall that hung in their brains; life-sized, she leaned over the sidewalk between the boarding houses and the train station, threatening to spill out of her blouse. In the morning, after a heavy rain, she steamed her own glass.

When it was finally time to go out on his first division run, Hugh knew very little about the train or his role on it but he had eaten well and seen several movies. At three in the morning he got out of bed with his heart pounding. He dressed carefully and warmly and was at the station early to put out on his first train. His division ran from Memphis to Paducah, Kentucky, along a low shelf of land where the Cumberland and the Ohio Rivers join together above Kentucky Lake and Lake Barkley. He was to memorize every turn along this route, every change in grade, until he knew it by heart.

The firelighter stepped down from his post between the cab and the tender just as Hugh arrived. The sweat was running off the boy's face, the coal-gray undershirt clinging to his wet torso. "She's awake and hungry," he said, and grinned at Hugh, who stood on the platform with Isaiah's heavy wool coat tucked under his arm. The boy's teeth were brilliantly white against the soot-stained skin of his face. In his mouth Hugh had the cigar he had bought for a nickel the night before, thinking he would smoke it like Jesse James as the train rolled out in the cold morning air. He put the cigar in his breast pocket when he saw the firelighter jump down from the platform to the tracks and cross between several chipper cars to another cold engine. The firelighter disappeared into the dark of the train yard, appearing again farther off, a small silhouette staring into a young fire. It produced in Hugh a misgiving that he did not have time to consider.

The first engineer called out to him as he stood wondering what to do with himself. The engineer to Paducah was a short squat man with a barrel chest. Dark hair grew high on his neck out of the open collar of his shirt. He had a cigarette dangling from his lips that he puffed on without touching as he made his way down to Hugh. Smoke poured out of him as he spoke and seemed to keep coming out of him well after he had spit the cigarette down between the rails.

"You my handle?" he asked.

"Sir?"

"You my handle to Paducah?"

"I'm a fireman."

"You're a hickory handle is what you are, son. First stop is in Milan at the plant. We come in there real slow so don't kill yourself, 'cause after that it's several climbs to Paducah up that limestone. I'll need you to keep it hot all the way up. Only back it off when I say. The machine stoker on this one is jammed so don't go jimmying with it. You'll only make it worse. It ain't worth a shit even when it works anyhow." He slapped the side of the auto-stoker shoot violently, as if to prove it was broken. "Just run that handle when I say and don't when I say don't. That's all you here to do, run that scoop handle. And make sure we got sand in that dome, at all times. Every time we pull out, check it."

"Yes sir," Hugh said.

"You put your stuff up here in the cab."

Hugh put his coat on a rack against the wall inside the cab where the engineer had an ICR uniform hanging.

"Will I get one of these?"

"No. You won't need one," the engineer said, grinning.

He stood there wondering what else the man would say.

"Want to put that shirt up?" the man asked.

It was a chilly morning and Hugh did not want to get out of his shirt. He hesitated and then finally took it off, now standing in his undershirt.

"Didn't they show you where to stand?"

"Yes, sir."

"All right then."

The engineer turned and got back to looking at some papers as Hugh went around to stand in his place between the engine and the tender.

The heat before the engine was exotic. Tremendous. Hugh couldn't breathe. When he pulled the hatch on the grate the heat bloomed as it got some air. His eyes watered and the water dried instantly and they burned and he shut them tight. He thought he would pass out and die. Jesus, Sweet Jesus in hell, he thought. Vivid colors glowed behind his closed eyes. It was as if the boy he had seen, the one who had started this fire, had walked miraculously out of the flames like Shadrach in the Bible. He did not have the same magic. He could not do this, he thought. He stepped back onto the floorboard away from the grate and took a big breath.

"Stoke her some," yelled the engineer. The drive-wheels huffed forward and slung him down the floorboard a few steps until he found the handrail. He stepped back into the blaze and felt his skin grow soft. He turned his face from the grate and gasped and found the firemen's goggles hanging on the post. He threw them on. He began stoking as the train moved, realizing now that if he stood still for too long while the grate was open, for even a moment, his arm would burn. He threw the leather apron on. He put on the leather arm bands and the heavy gloves. He would have to trade sides, trade arms. Still, the heat was astonishing and somehow growing worse.

The drive-wheels lurched hard as they got traction and he fell backward into the tender bunker and came out with a fresh cut on the back of his head. He put the gloved hand back there and it came back bloody and covered in coal dust. When he got his feet under him again he spread them out and learned to keep them spread, front to back, and to keep his knees bent. His head was throbbing. He stoked as the engineer called to him and they developed the slightest bit of momentum, imperceptible, and then they were moving and the calls for stoking came regularly.

The hickory scoop had a wide mouth and could tote fifteen pounds of coal in one scoop, enough weight to make his back cinch tight with pain in only a few minutes. He bent his legs when he could no longer move his back and his legs burned and he started thinking about water and an eternity passed with that single thought on his mind. Amidst the motion of his body, which went on magically without his will after his will had given out, that single thought rang like a bell clapper. Two notes. Water. He had not brought any. No one had told him to bring any.

It now occurred to him how little a half-dollar is and how long a day can be and how many hours can fit into such a long day, and how many minutes fit into an hour, and how many seconds in a minute. The sheer weight of time came down on him like an illness and tortured his mind and everything was permeated by that sickness.

When they came over the hill through the Hatchie Forest he had soaked through his undershirt and his arms and legs trembled. The engineer called him off the stoker. They would coast into Milan.

Day had come though it was still early. He stood out on the footboard and watched as river-bottom stands of bald cypress and oak gave way to fields throbbing with green light. The body of the engine was alive with exhaust. Undulant scenes played in the hot air in front of the train as the side rods pawed the wheels over with loud explosions of steam. A blue fog hung on the hills, slinking down beneath them through the creek beds as they passed over low bridges. He pulled off his gloves and found several large blisters on both palms. He could not make a fist, nor could he open them fully. The hands were fixed around the ghost of the scoop handle.

He went to the cab and found the engineer standing by the window with a serious mad expression, listening out for torpedoes on the rails, looking into the fog ahead as if he could penetrate it like a seer. There was a jug of water on the floor with a stopper in it. Hugh seized on it without caring whose it was. He held the jug up to his face and drank for several minutes. He could feel his hardened throat take a normal softer shape again. It was easier now to breathe and swallow. After a few minutes watching the engineer, he slid his cigar out of the shirt hanging by his wool coat and took it back with him out on the footboard. He lit it on the face of the closed grate as the brakes gave their first whines.

A pair of tall gates swung back as they pulled into the Milan Arsenal Plant. A man in a uniform stood on a long wooden platform where they paused. He jumped onto the train and went into the cab with some papers, came out laughing. The engineer was laughing too.

"Can't smoke in the plant," he said when he saw Hugh.

Hugh took the cigar out of his mouth and looked down at it. It was a good one, had cost him five cents and he intended to smoke the entire thing.

"You toss that thing 'fore we get through this next gate."

"But this whole train is breathing fire."

"You toss it."

"I can't have a cigar in there?"

"Hell no you can't. You can't smoke in this plant."

Hugh threw the cigar out onto the platform where the man had been standing. It sparked as it landed and rolled into a gap in the decking but did not fall through.

"Boy you got started on the wrong foot and you're still on it. Who do you think you are, Wyatt Earp?" The engineer and the gate man began to laugh.

The coat, he thought. He might as well have come out wearing a suit and tie. He had never been the butt of a joke before. His mind flared with anger. He was beyond exhausted and his head ached from striking the tinder box. He went into the cab and got his coat off the hook. He put it on and stepped down to the tracks and began walking alongside the cars. He would walk the line back through the forest and then hitch rides to Memphis. The idea of walking in the cool air strengthened him. He could walk all day, he thought.

"Where the hell you going, hickory stick?" the engineer yelled.

"I quit," Hugh yelled back.

"You won't get paid a half-trip."

Hugh kept walking.

"You leave me here without a stoker and you'll never work for us again," the engineer yelled.

But he knew all that. He knew he was done the moment he saw the firelighter coming down from the engine, scurrying off with his black face between the chipper cars; it had just taken him the morning to realize what he had seen.

———

There was a sign in the door of a pool hall on Beale Street for a waiter. The place served a ten-cent bowl of chili as large as a washbasin. They opened at ten in the morning and served until ten at night. They were busy in that time before the war and saw many of the customers seven days a week. The man behind the bar handed Hugh an apron the moment he walked in the door and told him he would make a dollar a day and get free meals.

"The kitchen gets pretty warm during the day, would you mind?" asked the man. "Hell no," Hugh said.

He stayed on for a year. The man he met behind the bar happened to be the sole owner of the place. His name was Frank Thomas. He was a bald man in his late forties with a heavy mustache. Hugh liked him immediately. He had recently become a Christian, he told Hugh their first shift together, and he claimed to have been a professional pool player before he became a convert and, thereafter, a chili cook. Hugh did not pursue him on the connection between chili and Christianity but it was such idiosyncrasies, stated as foregone conclusions, that endeared the man to him.

Hugh spent most of his time at the restaurant. He woke up early and ate his breakfast there for free and stayed late into the evenings. He left occasionally to watch a movie, or walk around by the river, but he preferred to be beside Frank behind the counter, watching men come in, listening to their stories.

One night after they had closed down the kitchen he watched as Frank ran a few racks of nine ball. He did it as if it were merely another mess he was cleaning up. He put up his pool cue with a smug look on his face. Hugh knew instantly on seeing this that it marked the beginning of something for him.

"You thought I was pulling your leg?" Frank said.

"Maybe I did. Can you teach me to do that?"

"Hell no," Frank said. "It ain't Christian."

"Who said I was Christian?"

After that night Hugh would often ask Frank to play and he would if there was a free table and no one was at the counter. Frank was full of stories and advice about the game. He loved to talk and seemed to forget in these moments that Hugh was on the clock. Hugh watched the choices Frank made and discovered in time an almost occult logic behind each one. Frank showed him some things—how to grip the cue, where exactly to strike the ball—but he always said in the end that the game couldn't be taught. It was in the eye. Either you saw it or you didn't.

Hugh could see it. Not at first, but soon enough. They now played for hours each night after the kitchen closed and over the course of that year he came to see a great deal.

Soon Hugh realized he could make twice the money playing for a few hours after the kitchen closed than he could working all day. Frank watched him start to win from behind the bar as he cleaned up for the night. He watched him on those nights with a quiet and remote recognition, as if he were standing on a riverbank, watching a swift silent current.

After a year at Frank's, Hugh decided he would quit serving tables and spend his evenings walking between the various pool halls in Memphis. Frank told him he couldn't serve chili for the rest of his life but that pool wasn't a replacement.

"You got to find your path," he said. "Or maybe you might think of enlisting. Why don't you enlist now, before you don't have a choice?"

Hugh told him he wanted to see if he could save some

money, get ahead for a bit. "It's not bad, or against God, to play pool."

"You can't win at pool," Frank told him. "It's not a winning game."

"I'm not old enough to enlist."

"How old are you?" he asked.

"Seventeen."

"Well, you can't win at pool," he said again.

"It's better if I don't win, not all of 'em. I just need to win at the right ones," Hugh said.

"That's not what I mean."

"What did you mean?" But Frank had gone back to making his chili. Hugh had disappointed him in this, he knew that. He put his hand out to say goodbye but Frank did not look up.

Several bars and diners kept tables in the back and some stayed open all night long. Roy's was a good place for his time because it was on the water and full of men who were traveling on the river. He got better odds. The downside to good odds was that it was a rougher place. Unlike Frank's, Roy's served cheap beer and most of the men came to drink and did so heavily. The crowd was often loose, and many nights there was some fighting near the tables.

Many men were drunk before they entered the room, coming from places that had turned them out or closed down. The smell of their breath was close in the heat of summer and it came to smell like money. He could only take so much off of them. After a few games they would treat him like a novelty; they paid him pocket change to run nine ball. He would throw out a number, the sets he could run, and they would bet against him and gather friends to watch. They would call out crude things and tell him lewd stories, hoping to distract him if he got to the last set. "I had a girl once in Arkansas. You know what she loved to do sometimes. . . ."

Another set of players were like him, younger men who had learned, as he had, to conceal their talent. They brought a desperate edge into the room when they came. They could look very drunk but it was hard to tell. He tried to steer away from this sort of player but sometimes he could not. Sometimes they came hoping he would be there and if they came to find him they wanted to bet on territory, not money. A loss meant you never came back to that place. These were the players that made Hugh nervous, volatile and strange, their ages uncertain.

Once, in the spring of that year, he saw how easy it could be: He'd played two games with a tall heavyset man wearing alligator shoes. He seemed worth some money and was looking for a game. He seemed cocky too, and Hugh liked the type. Hugh's shots were made to look sloppy; they went in, but just barely. His art was to make it appear as if his luck was being exhausted on every shot, as if it were about to expire.

That was the difference between him and the other players: where the others might let their opponents win a game or two early on to get the odds they wanted, Hugh had a different strategy. He played against his opponent's shame, knowing that shame could motivate. The shame of losing over and over again to such a lucky and untalented player. That was the angle. And then there was the added shame of watching a child put large bills into his pants pocket like he was innocent, like he was selling lemonade.

At the end of the third game, instead of handing over the last of his money, the heavy man in alligator boots took the cue ball in hand and threw it into a tall mirrored sign hanging on the wall outside the bathroom. The glass exploded and the tone of the room shifted down, took on a new edge.

"You little shit," he said. "You're gonna give me *all* my money back."

He approached quickly and Hugh was frozen, considering the man's size, the weight of his massive shoulders, the bulk of his left arm as it cocked back. Hugh tried to step back, to turn with the punch as it came, but this was not his game. He had never been in a fight before.

The man dropped his left shoulder but the heavy fist came across from the right so that as Hugh moved to dodge he only turned his head into the force of the blow. It was a cunning move. Alligator Shoes was not without talent. As the fist connected fully with the left side of Hugh's jaw a river of blue sulphur blazed up inside his skull. For a moment he was swimming in blue heat and then the bar became a very dim and distant place. He could feel the muscles in his legs spasm behind his knees and then he felt the muscles ease and then he couldn't feel them at all. The floor came up to him. He rolled onto his back in time to see the man moving up beside him.

He took a hard kick under his arm and felt the air in his lungs go out, heard a dull crack in his ribs. He rolled beneath the table as the bottom of the man's boot scuffed his hip. His head crowded with pain in his jaw, in his side; he couldn't get air. The man drug him out from beneath the table by his pant leg and Hugh saw a short knife flicker in the fat right hand. The blade gleamed, terribly.

Hugh kicked at the man's crotch from the floor and kept kicking, frantically trying to keep him back but his mind was only on the knife. Though the man was large he moved with unthinkable speed. The knife winked again in the bar light and then switched hands. The man's face shined with purpose and dark knowledge and Hugh knew he had stayed too long in Memphis, that he should never have come. He recognized suddenly that he was only a child.

The knife came down across his stomach. He squirmed and sucked in his gut and slid backwards across the floor. The blade moved across his skin again but this time he felt no pain. He could see his father on the Heloise ferry, could see his father's smile, the broad sharp nose, the dark skin, the eyes of Pathkiller in his father's face, staring at him from across the generations.

The man had him by his hair. Hugh threw a weak punch into his ear and then his arm was under the man's left boot. He saw the knife gleam and felt his head cocking back like a young bird's when the man came down on him, his tremendous weight like an embrace. The knife skittered across the floor where it struck the base of a chair and spun to a numinous stop like a dowsing rod.

A hatchet had come, a tomahawk humming in the air, falling out of a gap in time to save him. His blood had come; Pathkiller had come; something had saved him from Alligator Shoes. No, he thought, he had already died and was dreaming.

A figure stood above him. The barman, one hand choking up on a short wooden bat.

"Did he stick you?" the barman said.

Hugh couldn't say. He didn't know. He rested his head on the ground and tried to breathe. His stomach felt slick and hot. Was he bleeding? The room dimmed, pulsed, and then appeared again.

"Goddammit," the barman said, looking into the heavy

man's hair for blood. It was coming now. Just by Hugh's shoulder. The blood poured out, dark like grease. As it met the sawdust that lay on the floor it mixed into a rich rosin. The barman rolled the heavy man off and examined Hugh. There was a long opening in his shirttail, a bright line etched on his brass belt buckle and an opening in his right pant leg that exposed the inside of his pocket. The roll of money was cut, layered like the leaves of a cigar.

"You lucky son of a bitch," the barman said.

Hugh lifted his head to look and as he put his head back down the bar dimmed finally and completely and he fell off away from himself through the floor, through himself, through the deepest forms of regret and relief and then into nothing and he left behind the terrible pain in his side and in his jaw and he was grateful to leave it.

He woke in the back of a patrol car. A tube of ammonia had been broken beneath his nose and if he wasn't dead yet he thought the ammonia would finish him off. His head throbbed, a bulb of pain waking in waves. He wasn't completely awake but he still fought frantically against the hand that pressed the substance under his nose. He took a deep breath and that ignited the pain in his side and still he swatted the air before him blindly.

"That's it. That's all," said the officer. Hugh was slow getting up from the backseat, slower still getting the bright images around him to dim so that he could make them out. The police officer was a short fat man with tiny little eyes that seemed stuck in a smile. A doctor met them in a small examination room at the bond jail and told him his jaw was not broken but one of his ribs might be. He was made to stay the night in a cell so he could give a statement on behalf of the barman in the morning when the office opened. "In case the big fella shouldn't make it," said the fat officer. The doctor came back early in the morning and tapped on his chest, his ribs. He listened to his breath move easily in and out of him and then he wrapped him up beneath his arm in gauze so tight he could finally breathe against the pain and it was a welcomed close feeling.

He told the investigator what he could but it was all a formality. A stenographer fired away on a tall Underwood while he spoke. The man had a knife and the bar man struck the man with the knife. He, still wearing the opened shirt and ripped pants, needed only to sign his name at the bottom of the form. "Write 'luckiest man alive,'" the clerk said, smiling as he passed the form across the table to Hugh. He handed him the wad of cut cash. Hugh felt he might get sick looking at it.

The bond warden came in around ten and paraded him around. He took him up to cells full of drunks, men waiting on court dates, men who had no money for the fines and would be out after their trials with time already served. The warden had already told the story. The men came close to see the belt buckle with its brightly gleamed valley.

One old Quapaw man with deep-set eyes peered at him from the back of a single cell. His mouth hung slightly open, his dry lips like a gash across his face. He reached out quietly through the bars and ran his fingers down the line in the belt buckle as if he were tracing a path on a map. He seemed very sad. He traced for Hugh a line in his own large gnarly palm, another across the back of his hand, another across his cheek. He pointed again at the gash in the buckle of the belt and swatted Hugh's cut shirt and raised his palms. He shook his head, a raw look on the heavy face, a worried look. He spoke in his own language, and not to Hugh, or to the warden, but to himself, a story he held in his mind.

"Don't listen to this old Cherokee," said the bond warden. "He only makes sense when he wants to. When he sees the judge he starts making sense. You ought to hear his English then, make you think he memorized the whole dictionary."

But Hugh wanted to hear the man; he wanted the man to speak. I have no scar, he thought. What will they say, a young man who tells a story but has no scar? Again, the Quapaw man motioned at the belt buckle in disgust and Hugh felt like a pile of ash; he felt the gust from the man's thick hand blowing him down. I am too high above the river, too immune to the world to tell its story. Even if he could speak the man's language the message would not distill into words.

In his mind he saw the long line of men whose money he had taken; he saw the firelighter scrambling down from his engines—a curse he thought he could escape, to not stoop so low as that boy, but he could not. He could see an already tired future stretching out endlessly in front of him like the gleaming rails of a train, a long strand of trite, slick, purposeless, knowledgeless moments, not adding up to a life but to a kind of not-living. He had forgotten his life with Isaiah and Della; he had forgotten his father, his sister; he had been greedy, and lonely; he had committed the sin of loneliness.

He walked down the block toward his boarding house, emptied of his recklessness and scared. That night in the boarding house he wept because he longed to see his sister. He had been returned by the Quapaw man to a kind of boyhood. Fear invaded his mind from every direction and even the bareness of the room scared him. His loneliness was without limit, as if it had been accumulating for years, following him, and had only now just caught up to him.

He packed up his things, staging them by the door for an early exit, and slipped his rent for that month under the door of the landlady's room. He slept poorly on top of the made bed in all his clothes. The next morning he dropped Frank a note—who's to tell them I'm not eighteen, it said—and was at the Navy office before it opened, waiting through the interregnum of night on his grandfather's luggage, swallowed in his grandfather's big wool coat, when the light of day is like the kingdom of God that came and is coming and has not yet come.

Year of the Champion Trees

Myself and fear were born twins.
—Thomas Hobbes

OUR RHYTHM WAS BIMONTHLY. One of us would call and ask the other a question. *Have you heard about this new thing where people domesticate foxes?* Then two months would go by and it would happen again. It was our way with one another, an unspoken pact between brothers not to talk about anything important.

The last time we spoke it was about the shelf-life of medications, if they can really go bad. John thought the drug companies put something in to make the compounds unstable, a self-destruct chemical.

"Like Lamarck?" I asked.

"Lamarck?

"Like use it or lose it?"

"Yeah," he said, "like that."

That was back in September. We were overdue by a few days when his boss called the house and spoke for a while with Mom.

"Have you heard from your brother lately?" she asked me. She hung the phone back on the wall and had to turn around several times to get out of the cord.

"No, not for a while."

"When's the last you heard?"

His supervisor said it wasn't like John to miss days and that he was concerned. We called his phone and got nothing. We drove to his place that evening and his car wasn't there. We got the owner on the phone and waited twenty minutes for her to let us in. She tried several keys. Mom took big breaths between each key while Dad kept knocking on the door, as if John were in trouble now.

The apartment was tidy, nothing packed or altered. The only thing of note was that the heat was turned off. My brother and his efficiency. The thermostat blinked forty-four degrees. It made us cold looking at it.

We started calling around. No word from him in ten days to anyone. It took us a whole day calling to figure that out: grandparents, friends, distant aunts and uncles, second cousins, hospitals, anyone we could think of. And then Mom started calling random hotels and restaurants. "Have you seen a thirty-year-old white man?" she'd ask.

He could show up anywhere. I remember thinking that, the way loons travel such distances underwater. The wonder of those birds. The impossibility of their existence. The thought gave me a certain kind of joy. He was diving deep, sliding beneath the strata of his world. He could call from somewhere in the Midwest and tell us he was married. He could call from Florida and tell us he took a job as a parasail assistant. Somewhere on the surface of every possible option in life he would breach mightily like a whale. Any minute, this would happen. We would just have to wait.

The next day, the eleventh day, the sheriff's department pulled his cell phone data. It showed only one call the afternoon he went missing. He called the customer service number on the back of his credit card and had a long conversation with a woman at a call center in New Delhi. The center kept a copy of the entire conversation for "quality control." We spent day twelve waiting on a judge to issue them the subpoena. We sat in our living room as a family while the special-victims/missing-persons liaison played us the audio from her laptop.

The special-victims/missing-persons liaison was tall and thin with long blond hair. She wore a black suit and seemed like someone out of a fast-paced movie. She had a tall wave in her hair at the back of her head behind her bangs as if to conceal a terrible skull malformation. "Are you ready?" she asked us.

My brother's voice broke through to us, the audio thin and poor but the voice familiar. He sounded very calm. He told the girl that he was good at being quiet and good at waking up early in the morning. He was good at memorizing the names of plants and good at drinking coffee. Was he strangely happy to admit all this? He told her that when he is alone he imagines the questions he would like to be asked. He would like to be asked: who are the original members of the Miles Davis Quintet? He would like to be asked: what is the difference between a river and a paper birch, a maple and a sycamore?

The girl from the call center interrupted him to inform him about new cash-points on gas purchases at certain gas stations. He interjected to tell her how much he loved the world but that it was not enough. He said he would call her back later, when he felt better. "I'll call you back in a second," he said. She thanked him for being a valued customer.

"Does that suggest anything to you?" the liaison asked us.

We shook our heads. Shrugged our shoulders. No, we said. But this was not true. The phone call had suggested something to all of us, something we did not have words for, something very tall and cold and slow, the combination of a mountain and a wave, something very big coming down on us.

I wanted to tell the liaison everything I knew. I wanted to spill my guts: that my brother had always had fear in his blood, in his bones, and then deeper. What I mean is that he was the kind of kid who rode the bus to school in kindergarten with white knuckles around his umbrella stem, sweat on his brow. Other kids laughed or slept or made drawings on the foggy bus windows, but not John. He was my aspen, I wanted to tell her. He did not need the wind to tremble. He had it all inside him, enough wind to rip the siding off. The light of day scared him. Nighttime scared him. Sleeping scared him, but not as much as not being able to sleep; nothing was as scary as that.

On the thirteenth day his abandoned car showed up in an impound lot. It had been in the lot for almost two weeks after getting towed from a roadside in the upstate somewhere off Highway 25. The manager of the lot ran the tag and called us.

"Why did you wait so long to contact us?" Mom screamed. She was furious. She called the missing-persons unit to catch them up. Why hadn't they thought to check the impound lots? she asked them. "Why am I telling you this?" she said. They did not know what they were doing, she said, weeping. My father lowered her slowly to the carpet and lay down beside her and rubbed her back. I brought us all glasses of water and sipped mine slowly.

———

It was late November and cold in the upstate. The wrecker took us to the place. A narrow mountain road that hugs Little Gap Creek as it slides brightly down the long granite slabs. My brother liked coming up here. I remember that. He liked the Poinsett bridge that clung to the mountain with its stone, its gothic arch, resting there as if it were a decision made over millennia like the mountains themselves. The cops pulled off in front of us, their lights like slung dolerite, oscillations against the wet rock.

We got out of our cars and listened to the running creek and shivered in the early morning. Kennels were opened and cadaver dogs slipped up the hills. They combed the hair of Callahan Mountain, baying and vanishing into the viburnum, hobbling here and there and turning and then running strong again—all of them slick and thin and baying after the stained air. When the baying turned to barking and the barking gathered somewhere above us, somewhere on the mountain, a terrible stillness set in. The creek stopped running. The foggy steam froze over the road bed. The coroner and the police handlers walked slowly up the steep slope after the sound of the dogs, pushing their hands on their knees. My mother, who had been standing with my father near the back of the car, sat down cross-legged on the asphalt as if something heavy had fallen out of the sky and clocked her.

He had been missing fourteen days when they found him lying on the side of that mountain near a set of barrel hoops old as Prohibition, the staves rotted, given back. They found him lying in a constellation of ancient lycopodium. He would not have seen them in the dark, those pine mosses gathered around him; he would not have seen the barrel hoops or how, off to his right, above where he lay, a large tangle of boulders hung powerfully mid-fall, under a spell of stillness. It would have been too dark for him to see any of it. Maybe that made what he did possible. Or maybe the dark, coming every night all his life, had made it necessary. And he would only have felt the cold and seen the yellow line of the road growing thin and broken as it snaked beneath him and he climbed away from it.

I can see him climbing up the creek bed in the darkness of a new moon. His boots holding water, the pants soaked to the knee and heavy but it does not matter. Where the creek broke into two springs he took the left one for several paces. He exited the spring where it dogged down beneath some rocks and walked along the steep mountainside and lay down in a small depression, a lull in the incline between two large stones.

He would be one, even then, to have his special anxieties, his particular needs, to worry that his body would roll and somehow enter the road. Even from that height, even with the impossibility of it, the thought itself would have bothered him. He would not risk it, nor would he risk rolling once to face downward into the earth. He would not face the earth at all. He would face the stars, all wandering like a slow diaspora in the dark. He would lay himself between two large stones, tuck himself into the earth.

He had the pistol he bought in college and never shot except at the range. He had his wallet, his phone. He had his credit card tucked in the breast pocket of his shirt. He had his sourceless fear and confusion—always those things, he would never be without them—crowding out every other thing.

That night he smelled the wet rock and heard the Sabbath night ring slowly in the holy streams and he saw the stars turn as if he lived in the belly of a kaleidoscope and all of it confused and saddened him to completion and caused his heart to race as it always had all his life, to skip its strange beats, go all trochaic. And so he left it behind. And the pistol report rang like a bell in the mountain air and was trapped by valleys and in the morning the wrecker took his car away and erased him momentarily while the mountain held him up, bore him up like history.

I see his hair matted and full of leaves. I wonder if the sockets of his eyes held the rain, and if they were open and staring blankly through pools of water like lenses, in rapture, with nothing for all eternity to rub the strangeness from his eyes. I could not have seen this but it is worse for having not seen it. The factual is so easy to forget. The dream, impossible.

It was calendar winter in the South Carolina low country but still very warm. At my parents' church, heavyset men were wiping sweat out of their hairlines with the palms of their hands and wiping their palms on their pant legs. My shirt clung to my back beneath my coat. We were all crowded into a small wood-paneled church outside Beaufort. It had been many years since I had been inside a church building and I was auditing this experience from somewhere very near my body and so I remember everything. For instance: What is the source of two objects against each other—the sweat against my spine, my spine against a leaf, the leaf against my brother's back, his back against the moss, the moss against the earth? And who is the god of proximity? How can you pray?

Outside, somewhere nearby, a mile or so, the Salkehatchie River was bleeding into the St. Helena Sound and as it bled the breeze turned inland and the heavy brackish air moved over the water toward us. We ate barbeque sandwiches outside under a picnic shelter. I was starving and got seconds. Four devilled eggs like giant pills going down.

My mom walked around and spoke to everyone and Dad asked if they had all gotten enough to eat. There's plenty. There's plenty now, he said. He kept on repeating that. I watched as he fell into a kind of rhythm at the barbeque under the picnic shelter. He just needed to be a host, I think. He needed to be at a barbeque for a little while with some good friends who were all strangely overdressed. That is what he needed. That was his dream. As folks left to head to the burial service he spoke his usual goodbye to them, "Be good now. Be good," as if he were not about to follow them by police escort to the impossibility of our day, our new life where we are apparently alive and my brother is not.

As we drove to the burial service the cop's lights flashed in front of us for the second time and for the second time the flashing shook something loose in my eyes and I noticed the trees. *The trees*, I thought. There are so many of them. And I realized that I did not know their names. I would have to learn their names, I thought. This would be a kind of goodness. I would learn them. Each one of them. I would dedicate myself to knowing them. It would be an easy thing to do, and good. It would be a good thing to do. The year of the champion trees, a dedication. The year I would learn the joy of calling each thing by its proper name.

We buried my brother two days after we found him, sixteen days after he left his apartment near Clemson and died on the side of Callahan Mountain above the Poinsett Bridge. I moved back in with my parents in January of that year because I had quit my job and become an explorer.

I bought a cover for my truck bed and a small mattress and a stove and drove that truck all over the southeast looking for the biggest trees, the national champions. I would visit them all. The great alvaradoa in Dade, Florida. The cedar elm in Shelby, Tennessee. That year I divided god into a thousand tree-shaped images until I had outnumbered him. My new gods, my gods of naked seed, my champions—they surrounded him and dissolved his name like a breeze breaking against a tree line, like a child being shushed. Now I have given god a thousand new names, ten thousand new names, and I hold each name in my mouth, just to be close to it. I feel out the shapes of each name with my tongue and they are delicious musical things. Possumhaw. Larch. Hemlock. Oleander.

I learned that in Toombs, Georgia, there is an Ogeechee tupelo that is forty-five feet tall. In Coffee, Georgia, there is an eastern redcedar that is fifty-seven feet tall. In Congaree National Park there is a park ranger named Will Tallbreaker. Will is five-eleven and looks half-Cherokee. Will found me off-trail in the swamp looking for a champion sweetgum I had heard about but could not find. The tree was nominated that year and I wanted to know it. I wanted to tell the tree that I knew its name.

I had the tree marked on a trail map and walked off-trail for about a mile to where I thought it should be and it was not there. You can't hide a 185-foot tree. You can't hide something that magnificent. I hadn't walked straight enough, or far enough.

I was an explorer now and so I did my thing. I laid a big branch down in the direction of the trail and started making circles away from it. I circled twice to my right, one small and one wide and came back to the branch. No sweetgum. I circled out farther, this time to my left but it was too wide, or maybe it wasn't that it was too wide but more that it wasn't much of a circle, because I never got back to the branch. The trail was my broadside, the back-up, and so I started off toward it. After about fifteen minutes it all felt wrong. If I had guessed right I would have crossed the trail, and there had been no trail. My confidence waned and then suddenly disappeared and I felt my heart beating in my ears. I reversed myself again and went thirty minutes in the opposite direction, at least two miles, still hoping to broadside the trail somewhere and again found nothing. It occurred to me that I was lost in a bottomland forest the size of Brooklyn and that I would be spending the night there. I felt the earth shifting.

A series of realizations followed: My phone did not have reception and the battery was dying; I had not told anyone who knew me where I was going. I did not have a flashlight. In the dark, even if I walked all night, I would not be able to see the weak trail, I could cross it ten times and not see it in the darkness. I would somehow run into my older brother and for some reason he would try to kill me, he would take me with him and tell me how much he loved the world and how good he was at keeping secrets and he would try to kill me. I would run and fall into water and the water would be deeper than the world. The water would drink me.

I had not been paying attention to my walking but noticed now that it resembled more of a jog, and that I was running into limbs and that my arms burned and were bleeding. My walk slowed to a halt as I tried to get my head to clear. I tried to think of something smart to do and came up with nothing.

The light was so low the trees overhead were black against the dim blue and without dimension. The trees moaned beautifully and sexually in the shifting air, a chorus of groaning. I don't know how long I stood there but it grew completely dark. When I started walking again I was going very slow and falling often over vines. I was wet from all the falling and cold and moving slowly with a sort of despair, and then I heard the sound.

It was the sound of an ATV accelerating. And then I saw its lights winking in the breaks between the undergrowth in the distance and I screamed my head off. I screamed so loud my head felt like it was going to explode. "Hey," I yelled, and ran, and my voice broke I screamed so loud.

Will had been looking for me. My car was the only one left at the trail head and he was taking a pass through the swamp on the King Snake Trail just to give me one last shot—me, a stranger, being given a chance to be found. That's the kind of guy Will Tallbreaker is. When I saw the ATV stop and the big marine flashlight carve out the darkness I began to weep. It doesn't make sense—I wouldn't have died, but the fear was tremendous. I wept and I came to him in the beam of his light weeping like a child in a Walmart. Me, a twenty-eight-year-old man, soaked from falling in ankle-high water, filthy and weeping and running.

We rode down the trail slowly and my embarrassment clarified and deepened. I had gotten myself lost and cried when I was found, made myself into a parable. We stopped suddenly and Will pointed to a small herd of white-tails making their way across the trail out in front of us. They were beautiful and gray against the cypress knees. The last one to cross seemed to consider us briefly, poised, like us, in a kind of wonder.

"At night," Will said softly over the sputter of the engine, "the swamp is different. It wakes up."

"I'm sorry about earlier," I said.

"You're all right. That's all. You know. That's what I'm here for."

"Yeah. I'm glad you took one last trip. I would have spent the night out there."

"What were you doing out there?"

He pulled me around to my car. I was sipping an orange Gatorade he gave me at the ranger station and munching on a Powerbar that tasted slightly ferrous, like liver.

"I was looking for the big sweetgum."

He laughed. "Oh yeah. And who told you where to find it?

"Another ranger, I don't remember the name. She marked my map a few weeks ago. All the champions are on here."

I showed him the map. It was covered with small blue X's with the names beneath. Loblolly. Water hickory. Laurel oak. A pencil check mark beside the ones I had found.

"The sweetgum is hard to find."

"Why is it hard to find?"

"It's the farthest off-trail and it never seems to be where you left it. As the water rises the slough fills and the tree's distance off the slough seems to change. If you come back on Saturday I'll take you to it. We'll see if we can't find it. If it hasn't gone off on a little trip again."

"When? I'll be here."

"Come around nine."

"I'll do that."

"Be good," he said.

My tree was out there in the dark somewhere, so near to me that night I could feel it. I spent the week preparing myself mentally.

I helped Dad pick up pinecones in the backyard on Friday to pass the time. Anything to keep me busy. I remembered those days when I was a boy and could get half a penny for five cones. Dad was getting older and had learned to bend his knees. I tried to tell him about the tree I was going to see. How much John would have loved it.

"You ought to come with me," I told him. "It's beautiful out there."

"We have our basket-weaving class."

"Oh yeah," I said.

Since John died our kitchen table had been covered with coils of flat reed, ash splints, sea grass. This was their "intentional time" together, a part of their counseling. They had lessons every other Saturday. Dad was keen on the sea-grass baskets, and though he wasn't very good at it, I liked his baskets best. They had the cozy dishevelment of a bird's nest. Mom's baskets were made from round reed or split ash and looked like they could hold water. Her patterns were infinitely diverse: octagonal tiles, ropes stitched together, herringbone, shingled, all wound so tightly it was dizzying to look at them. I could see her perfect focus in the Saturday classes; I could see her avoiding my father's attempts at humor; her pain pressed up against the tip of her fingers, palpable and weave-able and profoundly complex.

Saturday morning I overslept. I had a dream that the champion tree cradled me like a child. I had another dream that it walked quietly on tiptoes across the cypress knees, always away from me, constantly vanishing into the gray languidness.

When I woke it was late, nearly nine. I floored it to the swamp. I tried to call the welcome center but no one picked up. I overheated my truck and had to pull over and let it cool so I could fill up the radiator. It was 9:50 when I finally arrived. I put my head in the door at the welcome center. Angie was sitting at the desk looking at her cell phone. She looked up at me and then back down at her phone.

"Hey, is Will around?" I asked.

"Will?"

"Will Tallbreaker."

"Yeah. He, like, doesn't work on Saturdays."

"Yeah. It's just that I was supposed to meet him a few minutes ago. An hour ago. I'm running late. I tried to call but no one picked up."

She looked down at the phone beside her on the desk.

"Huh," she said. "Yeah. I haven't seen him today." She stared across the lobby at the life-size Congaree Indian standing inside a diorama with a placid, plastic expression. They seemed to be staring at each other for a moment, both transfixed by the other.

"You can see if his truck's in the staff lot," she said.

"What kind of truck does he drive?"

"It's a big red one," she said, her hands up, like the truck was a fish.

I walked around the building to the staff parking lot and there was his truck, all big and red. I went back inside and borrowed a piece of paper and a pen and started writing him a note.

> Will,
> Please know how much I care. . . .

I tore the paper in half and put that piece in my pocket and started over.

> Will,
> Had car trouble. Tried to call the welcome center but couldn't get anyone. I'm going to hike for a bit to see if I can find you. If not, can we reschedule? It's important that I see the tree.
>
> Lewis

I stuck the note beneath his wiper blade and returned to Angie.

"Hey. Sorry to bother you about this."

"It's fine."

"Do you know, since he *is* here somewhere, where he might have gone to?"

"Let me see if he has his radio on."

She pulled a radio unit out from a charger on the desk and turned it on.

"Base to Will?" she asked it.

It answered with some soft hissing noises.

"Will?" she said again, "are you on?"

More hissing and then his voice appeared, a thick, heavy sound.

"This is Will."

"Someone's here. . . ."

"Lewis," I said.

"Lewis is here . . . to meet with you."

There was a moment of silence.

"Send him down to Wise."

She put the receiver back in its cradle and took out a park map and laid it in front of me.

"So he's on Wise Lake."

She circled the lake several times with a pen and tapped it.

"You head down the low boardwalk and take Weston loop trail and then take a right at the clearing over the bridge to Wise. Don't go left. It's to the right but you sorta stay straight."

"Got it," I said. And again, I was running.

When we were young my brother tried several times to teach me the size of the world. Even then he was alone with something, something I failed to grasp, the world itself perhaps, so familiar to me I could never see it.

"You see those stars," he asked. "Each one is larger than the sun, and each one is farther away than light can travel in like a million years, and each one is just as far from each other as we are from it."

"It's crazy," I said.

"It's impossible," he said.

"It can't be impossible, because it is. You mean it's impossible to understand?"

"No, it's just impossible. I don't believe it. It scares me."

I found Will taking soil samples around the lake. He was squatting down on his haunches poking at the mud. He washed his hands off in the lake water and stood and shook my hand. His hand was cold and wet and powerful like a fish.

"Thought you lost interest."

"No. Sorry. I got held up."

"That's fine," he said. He threaded the cap on a specimen jar and put it in his backpack.

"You still want to see it?"

"If you don't mind."

"Hell no. I'd like to see it again. Been too long."

We walked to the King Snake Trail and Will told me about the park, the outstanding diversity of life, the impossible number of living things on every level of reality. He sounded suddenly like my brother working under the burden of knowledge, or at the brink of it, unattainable. Everything here will shatter your mind if you let it. He told me he grew up in Arizona, in the high desert and became a ranger in the big western parks. He requested a transfer to the swamp after his first visit. He had never seen any place so beautiful, not anywhere.

"A swamp?" I asked.

"I know. But look at this," he said. He extended his hand out over a long slough full of water, the buttressed cypress and tupelo trees footed in their eternal reflections, mossy like mourners, the weeds of grief hanging on them like songs. He had a point. We stood listening to the trees moan.

———

I had not gone straight enough. The sloughs force you to zig-zag and a compass is needed to find your line again when you get around the water.

"See, I found you out here," Will said, pointing to a place on the map nearly a mile west of where he had the tree marked. "You moved around this first gut here and then changed your line with the water which took you out here. This place is a maze that changes week to week. Try taking us along this line."

He handed me the compass. I walked ahead, letting the occult little needle attenuate itself to nothing, to everything.

The tree was more treelike than in my dreams. That is to say, it did not walk away from me or cradle me like a child. I do believe, though, that it shuddered at my touch; I believe it knew my hand and heard me say its good old name. The bark plates were the matte gray of granite and vertically grooved. Spider mites moved in the deep furrows, racing upward in my shadow.

Its crown was tremendous above the canopy, greedy of light, having it first in the newness of morning, newness like the first hour of the world and then feasting in that newness without shadow through the long day. Be good, I said to the tree. Be good now. The light hurt my eyes as I looked up the trunk. It made me wobble, staring up that straight tower, the slow movement of the tree in the breeze causing my mind to compensate for a fall that was not happening. I stumbled back away from the tree as if struck by some terrible realization and fell backward into Will. He stood me up again by the shoulders. That's the kind of guy Will Tallbreaker is.

"You can take your hat off to this one," he said, "it's lived through centuries of hurricanes, fires, wars, you name it."

"And still here," I said, patting the tree on its side in congratulation.

"And still here," he said.

Will went to the back of the tree and put his hands around the bole and I did the same. We stretched our arms, our faces planted against the bark. We could hold one hand, but not the other.

They Were Calling to One Another

THE BANGS WERE HER DAUGHTER'S EIGHTH birthday present, the haircut she had begged for only to weep silently the entire car ride home, her mouth a quivering down-turned scar. She spent the rest of the day avoiding her reflection, giving herself the silent treatment.

Neighbors and classmates gathered at their house that afternoon for an under-the-sea-themed party. Ada sat sullen on the edge of the fireplace hearth, her new bangs pinned back against her scalp with barrettes while two twin brothers in matching fish costumes took turns punching the back of the sofa. The other kids watched in admiration.

Susannah ordered a birthday cake from Food Lion with a photograph of a seahorse printed on it. It looked like an impressionist version of the file she sent the baker the day before, a seahorse through a window on a rainy day. It had a shiny crumpled topcoat and reminded her of those times her mother forgot to take the wrappers off the Kraft cheese before making cheese toast in the oven.

She was grateful for the other mothers who dragged their children in the front door. Too grateful. "Thank you again for coming. It's so nice of you to come," she whispered, a lover-like passion in her voice, forgetting whom she had and had not thanked, not caring, drunk with appreciation that her strange daughter would not be alone on her birthday.

Susannah worried the moment the invitations went in the mail that no one would come. She knew her daughter did not make friends easily. She imagined her husband standing over the cake with a beer in hand, the two of them outlining the notes of "Happy Birthday," their adult voices heavy and careless with a song they did not want to be singing. Then Scott would tell her that he had to get back to Wilmington for a shift, that it was out of his hands—as he had the morning of Ada's actual birthday—and it would be mother and daughter, alone, unwrapping presents.

But these women had spared her that. Each time the doorbell rang she felt her eyes start to water. These kids were not the type with busy calendars, she could tell, but it did not matter. They were here unknowingly supporting each other, a banding together of outsiders. Their attendance represented an understanding between mothers, a communal warding-off of trauma. *These children of ours, one day they will realize they are of the Kool-Aid-mustache variety; they will grow suspicious of their clothing and how it does not hang right, how something about their posture is botched; how nothing flatters; they will not have the right things to say, or gestures, or voices; they will eventually come into the truth, they will walk into it backward: that no one is equal on the earth and that kindness is a rare and late style.*

Ada entered the kitchen that next morning with a victorious look on her face. She pulled up to the table and drank her juice. Susannah noticed Ada's forehead was somehow swollen, bulbous. She stared at it. *It*, or *them*? The missing bangs, a crescent of brown stubble on her child's brow like a fur covered headband. It was a rough job, a safety scissors' haircut.

"Well, look at you," Susannah said.

Ada touched the hair with the tips of her fingers, a worried look on her puffy face. Susannah unloaded some eggs on her plate and handed her the ketchup and watched her dig in. She went into the back bedroom and got the old dog clippers.

Ada did not protest as her mother stood her in the bathtub and went to work on her head. It was as if Ada knew this would be the final outcome, as if she had planned for it. Her shaved head made her eyes seem newly tremendous, gorgeous. Susannah noticed her daughter's eyelashes, their long languid batting, the Disney-like tremor. She was going to be a beautiful woman, a powerful thing in the world. *And what then?* Susannah thought. *When she is beautiful beyond doubt, how will I control her?*

A week later Susannah found the nest of cut hair crammed between the box spring and the mattress. The girl's room was warm in the afternoon, the air musky like crayons. She stuffed the hair in her jeans pocket and laid down on Ada's mattress, exhausted.

She could feel in the room the spirit of her daughter, stubborn beyond plausibility, pillow of coiled chain, lover of loneliness. She fell asleep thinking about a book her mother had given her two years before entitled *Raising the Willful Child*. She had never opened it.

Later that day, on the phone with her mother, Susannah asked, "Was I willful?"

"No," her mother said, "but her grandfather was. That's who she takes after."

Susannah's mother claimed to see it early on, this resemblance the girl bore to her grandfather.

"They don't look alike to me," she said.

"It doesn't matter. You can see it," her mother said. "You can see the gears turning. I know what that looks like."

This all seemed strangely Calvinistic to Susannah, darkly superstitious. She didn't share her mother's religious fervor and it made her uncomfortable to think Ada had something old and dormant lying inside her, something transferred across the ages.

"I need to go," she said. "The washer's shaking itself to death."

She hung up the phone and sat down on the toilet and read the back of a bottle of shampoo and tried to let the murky feeling clarify, to lift. Sodium laurel sulfate. Mint leaves extract. Rosemary oil. She popped the cap and took a whiff. It smelled medicinal.

She recalled one day waiting with Ada in a doctor's office. Ada was only five and already full of independence. Ada had spent that previous night with a spiking fever, trips to the bathtub to lie silent in cold water, Tylenol every four hours to keep her temperature below 103. Now they sat waiting to see the doctor and of course the girl was miraculously better, pacing the waiting room, and Susannah was an orb of exhaustion. She asked her daughter not to play with the water fountain, asked her nicely and then told her sternly and watched transfixed as the girl looked her in the eyes, a look of supreme innocence and unimpeachability, before turning to depress the valve.

Susannah had never imagined she would be one of those parents who gets walked all over in public. And yet, here she was. Smiling politely as Ada soaked her T-shirt, lapping at the stream of water just beyond the reach of her smug mouth, looking back at her mother joyfully.

Ada was ten when Susannah divorced her father. It had been in the works for two years. Scott had been working at the steel mill in Wilmington Island, living in an apartment out there all week instead of making the commute to Milledgeville twice a day. He eventually just stopped coming home on the weekends.

Later he called and said he met someone and Susannah was relieved. She had wanted it to be him to bow out, had wanted to be given freedom from the guilt of it all and she was grateful, in a practical way, for his taking the fall. When they told Ada she seemed indifferent to their story. They had carefully prepared their remarks, had solicited advice from professionals about the nature and consequences of this moment in a child's life. But it was as if they had interrupted her important day to convey some tedious aspect of adult life. Her bare feet dangled off the edge of the sofa a few inches above the carpet, the heels touching.

The next morning Susannah came back inside after checking the mail to find all the kitchen drawers pulled out, turned over on the kitchen floor. Silverware strewn beneath the refrigerator, gleaming in the dark mossy space by her toes. Ada was not in her room. The back bedroom door was locked. Susannah pounded on it. Demanded it be opened. She went over to the neighbor's trailer and returned with their seventeen-year-old son, a boy nicknamed Buckwheat. He was an obese teenage boy who must have weighed at least 290 pounds, a boy who spent most of his afternoons pushing a defensive line sled back and forth across their backyard while his father, who was also his coach, screamed things at him. Father and son, fiercely devoted to one another, fierce red faces, screaming and embracing. A working relationship. She envied them.

Susannah yelled again through the door with Buckwheat now standing beside her, grinning shamelessly, something dark, a bean skin maybe, stuck between his front teeth. There was still no answer. Susannah told Ada she was coming into the room and to stay away from the door.

"Okay?" she yelled again. "Stay away from the door."

Buckwheat seemed hesitant. Was he really being asked to break the door down? Susannah nodded. Buckwheat applied his shoulder to the door and it sprung open immediately, shattering the frame, the doorstop and the recess of the bolt. She could see Ada sitting in the closet, a pair of shoes exposed beneath the pants and dress shirts.

Buckwheat lingered for a moment, beaming and sweaty, his mouth wide open, the rasp of air moving through his proud face. Susannah thanked him and closed the broken door and heard him plod slowly out of the house.

The window curtains were shredded like country singer fringe. Ada had a paring knife at her feet. Her eyes were swollen and her face wet, her small jaw set for the ages. All the clothing in their closet was torn in strips like the curtains. Her husband's suit was mutilated, the sleeves gaping down to the wrist. Every piece of clothing, every blouse and dress like confetti but still attached to the hanger. Susannah picked Ada up and carried her over to the bed and lay down with the young girl still clinging to her. They fell asleep there, Ada's arms wrapped tight around her mother's waist.

———

In high school Ada possessed a severe kind of beauty, her figure small, lanky, her eyes still tremendous. She lacked the new revelations of her peers. She developed no sudden curves or protrusions. Only height. Her body was as androgynous as it had always been, the curves of her hips sharp, her breasts small cakes against her body. Still, to her own surprise, she began to receive attention from the boys. Her indifference to them proved provocative, gave them detectable pain. She liked this new world.

As a senior, she decided to have sex with one of them. She chose another outsider for the job. It was the boy who worked for his father on a car lot near their house. He was the kind of boy who seemed constantly unaware. He had a smooth, bland face like a baby's. His expression was distant, nearly vacant, and his mouth hung open when he walked, as if everything was a brainstorm, an impenetrable complication.

She persuaded him to steal one of the cars off his father's lot, which he did not want to do but did anyway. Susannah could imagine all of this, imagine how she worked him over slowly, carefully. It wasn't stealing, she would have reminded him, not when he already owned it, at least when his father did, and especially not when he planned to return it.

They snuck out late and met in the construction site of a home at the back of their neighborhood and waited for the timer to kill the lights. They drove all night without a license plate deep into the Haddock farmland outside Macon, down random dirt roads, along a field's edge. In the backseat of the stolen Cavalier Ada discovered that the boy knew the outline of what was to happen. The young man seemed possessed by some spirit, the way he panicked after her body, like a dreamer, greedy and scared to have the dream snatched away.

———

Susannah woke at six that morning with a police officer at her door, Ada in tow. The officer said he found them trespassing on an orchard in the backseat of a stolen vehicle. He said there might be charges.

Susannah asked what they'd been doing out there and Ada told her everything, as if to wound her. She felt her mind come off its axis, a deep longing for control. That night she tried to imagine what it was like for her daughter, the sun rising behind the gnarled boughs of the peach trees, the sun so new on the car's waxed hood. Did they drive down those rows through the tall grass, the spurred branches crawling with bees? Was there any regret, or fear? Susannah had by now imagined a thousand futures for her daughter, a thousand paths and personalities, and all of them seemed suddenly distant and subservient to the woman her daughter had already become, a lanky willful thing, with no need for her, or anyone, it seemed.

Ada disappeared for three days a few months after high school graduation—three days that drew out like an eternity for her mother, three days of imagining the girl's body strewn in the bahiagrass along 404. Susannah knew Ada had been spending some time with an older boy who worked at a detail shop, a tall half-Mexican-looking boy with a broad, handsome face. She tried not to imagine the two of them crossing the border some-where, entering the drug trade. *Was this racist?* she wondered. *Yes, maybe.* She did not care.

After the three days Susannah woke to the sound of a car door shutting. Ada was standing in the front yard in the early morning, leaving tracks in the dew, waving off a car full of young-looking girls. Susannah unlocked the door and lay down on the sofa, turned on the TV, tried to appear calm, maybe indifferent.

Ada entered, her chest wrapped in cellophane beneath her tank top. There was a tattoo of two exultant seraphim covering both sides of her chest. She stepped out of her shoes and kicked them beside the door and pulled off the tank top. As the shirt peeled back the black portentous figures appeared in full and Susannah felt nauseous. Now her daughter would forever be painted on, in dresses, in her wedding gown, forever marked up with some terrifying angel-demons.

"Well look at you," she said.

"It's a chest piece," Ada said proudly.

The skin was raised and red beneath the ink. The images extended down to Ada's lowest ribs. The seraphim's feet, arched back and pointed down as if in the first moments of flight, were partially covered by a pair of wings. Another set of wings swooped out in front of the seraphim's faces and converged directly between her small breasts, the wings almost touching tip to tip at the base of her neck.

"This is why you didn't call for three days? This is why I had the police out looking for you? To get some angels done on you?"

Ada stood in nothing but her jeans and the cellophane, her breasts flattened against her body like dough.

"Do you want to see it in the mirror?"

"I can see it just fine."

"The artist is going to take pictures of me when the swelling goes down. He did it for free."

"Pictures? Of your chest?"

"For his portfolio. It's art, Mom. That's why it was free."

Susnnah imagined Ada spread across the cover of a tattoo magazine at a truck stop, the ink menacing near the small buds of her nipples, the shallow dish of her sternum an empty spandrel, a gothic arch. It made Susannah feel like the floor was lifting, pitching forward. She went into the bathroom and covered her face in cold water and tried to calm down.

That night Susannah fell into a fitful sleep and dreamed the seraphim on her daughter's chest fell through the ceiling and landed in the bed, filling her mouth with black feathers, screeching like bats as they thrashed around in the sheets.

The next day in the grocery store Susannah stood with a wooden face before a potted white cyclamen, the cool sugared air from the flower case moving across her wrists, touching her plump thighs. When she was younger she had been skinny, lanky like her daughter. Now her legs touched above her knees, now the skin above her eyes was being slowly pulled down like shades, like hoods over her pupils. She thought of herself with incredulity, a botched attempt at motherhood. She thought of her mother's comments about her father—a man who ran away at fifteen, who spent half his life in prison, and who now lived several states away in a small apartment, always alone and somehow on the verge of mania. Could it be something inside them? Something he gave to her, like a spell. Did she inherit his will, his recklessness?

She stared at the tiny beads of water resting on the white petals and imagined Ada soaking in the bathtub at their first house. She saw an image of herself kneeling by the tub with a bar of soap in her hand, watching as the bath water turned an inky shade of blue. The seraphim on the sides of her daughter's chest turned hazy, the sharp contrast of the feathers and the powerful ominous arc of the wings dissolved and ran down over her daughter's ribs and into the water. Then there was only the dull shape, a faint outline on her sides and across the top of her breasts where the triumphant creatures had been, like a shadow and soon, with more soap, even that was gone completely and the pale skin seemed more perfect that usual. Her mother imagined kissing her ravenously, the backs of her hands, behind her ears. The bitter taste of soap. She saw the inky water running down into the drain, the dark line it would leave along the inside edge of the tub.

She bought the flowers because they were on sale and because she was embarrassed to think she had been staring at them for so long. She put them on top of the dresser in Ada's room. Ada was home, putting lotion on the new tattoo. Like a ritual, she anointed herself. It wasn't envy Susannah felt for this body but something else, something like possession. She knew as she looked at the sharp bones in her daughter's hips, the long elegant back and shoulders, the perfect bones at the base of her neck, that every cell had come from her, an offshoot, the young hand reaching out to grasp the ever-renewing world.

Susannah was staring at the tattoo now in the mirror, forcing herself to look at it, to accept it. She noticed then, as her daughter turned back toward the mirror, a thin script etched along the edge of both outstretched wings, language reaching toward language. Deciphered in the glass, two names, like the summons of an archway beneath the outstretched wings.

hannasuS—Susannah.

eniledA—Adeline.

A motherly dream? It must be, she thinks.

In the dream the mother says nothing about what she sees in the mirror. In the dream, the daughter sits in a chair before the mirror and the mother stands over her and takes up a hairbrush from the desk and brushes out the daughter's long dark hair. In the mirror that is the dream a two-headed creature looks back at them, and through them, forever calling out to itself, forever wondering just what it sees that makes it long for itself so deeply.

Swing Low Sweet Chicken Baby

WHEN ONE OF THE SUMMER HANDS LET a bucket of roofing nails get away—not yet learned enough to yell out as it hissed down the rake and disappeared over the collar beam—Bates was standing directly beneath, thinking about his sperm count and how he might get his wife to move back in.

The impact brought him down hard to his knees. He moved his fingers gently up his bald scalp, creeping along the gash. It started at the very top of his head and widened in the center as it slanted toward his right eye. He brought the hand back in front of his face and rubbed the blood between his thumb and forefinger like he would antifreeze or motor oil, testing the viscosity. The blood went thin with sweat and ran off the tip of his nose into the dust where each drop formed a small crater between his knees. Bates wondered if he could form his initials. He aimed the drops into the dirt with one eye closed, sighting off the end of his nose. He formed the L quickly, almost effortlessly, but found the B more difficult. The curves, they would be harder to get right.

———

Slowly, almost imperceptibly, Bates had grown to love his work. After twelve years he now woke in the morning with an ache in his chest that didn't leave until that first moment when his feet hit the dirt of the construction yard and he knew who he was. The owner of a roofing company.

His wife Ellen Louise had only been in Woodruff a year when they met, back when Bates was spraying herbicide for the Norfolk Southern Railway. She was known around town as the girl who sold makeup from her car. Bates approached her the very first time he saw her. She was standing behind her car in the vacant parking lot beside the tanning salon, fleshy arms flushed pink with the summer heat. She was wearing a white skirt with a slit halfway up the back. As Bates watched her from his truck window he felt the skin on the back of his neck prickle and grow warm, as though the midday sun were resting on it.

"You ever seen a truck like that before?" he started in.

She turned with her hair falling across her face, strands plastered to her wet forehead.

"That truck over there, the white one, with the gear on the front? You ever seen a truck like that before?"

"Am I not supposed to park here?" she asked. Bates suddenly found himself feeling sorry for her. It was her exhaustion, maybe, her tired trunk piled with boxes of makeup.

"That ain't no tow truck, girl. That's a railway truck. Ain't you seen a railway truck before?"

Bates spent the next few minutes telling her about the truck's features. She listened patiently, relieved that her car would not be towed because she didn't have the money to get it off the impound lot. He spent a few minutes more describing all the things he saw riding the truck at work. How good it felt to be away from the roads and traffic lights, out in the middle of nowhere, riding over bridges, crossing summer fields, the two parallel tracks in an endless convergence both before and behind. And somewhere in the midst of talking a change slinked across Ellen's face. She seemed to see him the way he might like to be seen by a woman: as someone who knew something about the world and how to get something out of it. The conception that Bates formed of himself in that moment, seeing himself that way through her eyes, was powerful. He fell in love with himself. They were married eight months later.

In time their marriage came to hang on the subtle problem of semantics. What Bates referred to as a *pyramid scheme* Ellen tenderly called an *in-home marketing career*. He would come home from work to find her on the phone, reading prompts from a notebook, winning devotees, and he drank more than usual to drown out the sound of her in the living room, talking to people about coupons and how she could change their life if they would but give her the chance.

They'd given up the hope of having a baby and neither would go to the doctor. One night, Bates overheard Ellen whispering on the phone to her mother. "*Herbicide*. With the railroad. No, I don't think he even knows. For, like, four years. I know. *I* know."

Bates had never considered this before. He lay in bed remembering the jolting service truck, the concentrated herbicide spilling onto his bare arms and hands, falling over onto

his shoes, soaking his socks. He remembered the thick gloves
that seemed pointless as the chemicals swirled in the updraft
of air behind the truck, a light mist falling down on him, a
sticky residue on the back of his neck.

"Ellen, it's either me or that goddamn pyramid scheme,"
Bates said one evening after nine years of marriage, pushing
the pamphlets off the edge of the table. They landed atop her
feet in a pile. She stepped back from the table and kicked them
against the base of the refrigerator and tromped off toward
her bedroom and started packing her things. Soon she was
gone, living again with her mother in a trailer somewhere outside Woodruff.

Bates found himself horribly distracted the week after Ellen's
leaving. He would be in the middle of a joist measurement,
counting rolls of underlayment, vaguely wondering about
the herbicide. The thought would sneak up on him amidst
other thoughts, appearing out of the most unrelated
details—the square footage of the flashing, the pitch of
the rake and the framing mistakes that would need to be
accounted for, the half-inch here, the full inch from that
twist to that hanger—and present itself shamefully until he
forgot where he was. The flash of trees, the sight of parallel
tracks gleaming, and then Ellen, a big round belly, turning
in a room painted pink.

That Thursday and for the first time since he could remember,
Bates cut out early to go to a doctor's appointment. A small
red-headed nurse at the desk watched him stomping his boots

outside on a rug that was too small, then dragging his heavy shadow across the tile floor. The nurse gave him a clipboard and a small plastic cup with a white threaded cap and led him to a bathroom down the hall.

It took Bates an unbearably long time to ejaculate. He occasionally looked down at the empty cup as he sat on the toilet inside the sterile bathroom, holding himself in one hand and the cup in the other. His arm shook as he tried to rouse himself, as if he were guiding a piece of grounding wire through a conduit. His mind continually fell away from him, spilling down through all kinds of absurdity. He tried to think about a girl he touched once between the legs during a movie in high school, tried to think about her a few years older, meeting her in a bar maybe and picking up where they left off; suddenly he could only remember the most vivid scenes from the movie itself. Then he thought about Clint Eastwood and the small cigars he always smoked and the way his upper lip would rise to a snarl as he moved the cigar into the corner of his mouth. Then he turned three shades of red and had to start all over again. Twenty-five minutes had gone by and Bates was sweating profusely, the back of his thighs wet on the lid of the toilet seat. He had almost given up and was preparing in his mind to just leave when the nurse knocked on the door to ask him if he needed anything. The embarrassment of the question was enough. He quickly snatched the cup, which was sitting on the edge of the sink, and bent himself down into it. "No'm," he quivered.

That evening Bates stood in front of his kitchen window watching as the cars passed by on 86, watching the heat crinkle the air over the asphalt and feeling the beer he'd been drinking make his lips numb. The cicadas droned in the yard outside the window as he leaned his forehead against the pane.

In the garage he found a bag of frozen chicken breasts in the storage freezer and brought it snugly up against his chest. He rested his head against the frozen chicken and rocked it back and forth, intuitively shifting his weight between his feet. He applied only the smallest amounts of pressure to the freezer bag. He understood its weight, as if he were intimately familiar with it, as if he had picked it up a thousand times a day.

He closed his eyes and began to sing softly beneath his breath, bobbing the bag up and down in his arms as he made small orbits on the floor of the garage. He liked how his feet made soft, tacky sounds in rhythm. *Crows in the garden pullin' up the corn. Gardener asleep in the shade of the barn. Wake him, wake him, tickle him and shake him. Crows in the garden pullin' up the corn.*

An hour later Bates and the bag of frozen chicken were asleep together in the imitation Barcalounger. They stayed in that position all night long while on the TV an infomercial about a collapsible ladder cast a strange wavelength of blue over the couple. The light fell on Bates' face and made his skin pale and sickly. It fell into his open mouth and made his lips appear purple and his teeth glow green. It produced an oblique square in the glass eye of an eight-point buck that was mounted with great pomp over the fireplace mantle.

In the morning Bates woke with the thawed chicken tucked carefully in the cleft of his shoulder. The freezer bag was leaking a good bit by then and the fatty chicken water had run down, soaking his armpit, his side, and his lower back, pooling beneath him in the leather recesses of the chair. Bates walked with it against his chest into the garage and then used both hands to carefully lower the chicken into the large freezer, positioning it between a flank of deer venison and a few bags of peas. He changed his shirt, which smelled of sweat and chicken fat and when he left the house for work the freezer lid in the garage was propped open with a spent shot gun shell to ensure that the light would stay on inside.

Later that morning Bates' phone rang as he was yelling at a summer hand, the same hand who would let the nail bucket go without warning.

"Who laid this corner of flashing?" Bates barked. The boy didn't answer. He had a bright piece of flashing in his hand and was trimming it out to fit a drain vent. He shrugged, as if to say, Who could ever know such things, such mysteries? Bates shook his head at the boy.

The number of the fertility clinic blinked on his cell phone. It was still early in the day. His senses seemed suddenly clarified and deepened. Bates flipped open the phone and envisioned the nurse smiling as she told him; his sample was fine. There was nothing wrong with him.

One of the other full-timers heard the summer hand on the roof shouting for someone to retrieve the nail pack. He quit the circular saw in the middle of a long piece of plywood and walked around to the back of the house. It was there that he found Bates, on his knees with his head sunk, dripping someone's name into the sand.

Father Brother Keeper

S HE DID IT WITH HIS FATHER'S OLD ELECTRIC clippers. Pressed steel. 1950s heavy. He knew the sound of them by heart. Flip the switch and the clippers dim the lights and moan like a lover, oscillate like a hive.

It was midday and there was nothing going on in the house. He'd been lying on a mattress in the alcove for an hour since waking, listening to the AC unit rattle in the frame of the window above his head. He heard the clippers going and thought he might get up, see what Elsie was doing.

In the bathroom he found his sister-in-law with her head half bald, the sink full of thick black hair. What hadn't been shaved was teased into a fro. She looked like a dandelion half-blown, a love-me / love-me-not, a question mark of love.

"You crazy," he said to her.

He'd only been living with his brother and Elsie for a month, and if he'd learned anything that month it was that he did not know her. Everything she did and said caught him off balance.

She plowed the clippers up the near side of her head. A swath of brown scalp appeared and then another. He thought he'd leave the doorway, go back to his own business, but he could not. He wanted to watch this.

She was almost done when she turned off the clippers and faced him, her head bald except at the back, a strange mullet appearing in the mirror behind her.

"You just gonna keep standing there watching?"

"I need to pee."

"Well go on."

"With you in here?"

"I'm not leaving my own bathroom, so you just go if you have to go."

He stepped around her. It took him awhile to get started.

"Can you keep a secret?" she asked, leaning over the sink to peer at the thing in his hands. He shook himself and felt her gaze on his body, felt her eyes taking him in.

"I don't know. I guess it depends."

"Everything depends with you, don't it? What does it depend on?"

She crossed her arms and he felt suddenly that he was negotiating with a chieftain, a cult leader, the mullet her vestment. One wrong move, one misstep, and the priests come with knives made from iridescent shells. The gods cry blood in old, forgotten languages.

"Who I'm keeping it from, I guess."

"From everyone. That's what a secret is."

"Okay," he said.

"Nevermind," she said.

The clippers moaned again. She went after the mullet but couldn't reach it. She only made it thinner, a little off-center, meaner. He turned to go lay down again when she called him back.

"Hey," she said, "I'm pregnant."

"For real?" he asked.

"Yeah. Would you do the back?"

She put the clippers in his palm and the weight felt so right, like holding time itself. And the way they hovered just over his hand as they vibrated, the way they jolted like the body of a bluegill trying to slip back home, that felt right, too.

For several years his father had been a barber. That was when they lived up in Memphis. Micah had spent his childhood afternoons playing on the cold tile of his father's shop, listening to the sound of men's voices clattering against the hard surfaces. The cigarette smoke contorted upward between the mirrors on the front and back wall, the movement shrinking in both directions for eternity, becoming eternally small, or just far. The distance the light traveled in that shop during the day between those mirrors? Who could say? Fifteen feet to the power of infinity? And yet the men laughed in that gap, their own heads turning into upward curving lines that ran in two directions for all of eternity. Micah saw something in this as a boy that he could not articulate, saw that each event, each moment, had extensions that could not be stopped, that nothing could be brought back again.

He studied his sister-in-law's face in the bathroom mirror. She was serious. She was pregnant. She leaned down and stretched her neck over the edge of the sink like it was a chopping block, exposing the arched bones at the base of her skull. They were elegant. He had not noticed this before when her hair was long, the long elegant neck. He ran the clippers slowly up the back of her head and blew the cut hair off her nape. He wiped her head and neck with his fingers, felt how smooth it was in one direction, how rough in the other.

"Done," he said.

She stood and eyed him for a moment in the mirror.

"Why you doing this?" he asked her.

"'Cause I'm pregnant," she said.

"Yeah, but why?"

"I just told you."

"Issah doesn't know yet?" he asked.

"I'm a tell him when he needs to know."

"All right then," he said.

He put the clippers back in their leather bag. It smelled like 3-in-One oil and made his head swim back twenty years. Elsie began to sweep the floor. He picked a lock of her hair up off the tile and twisted it into a cord and then tied the cord in a knot. He put the little bow of hair on the edge of the sink like a gift and watched her rub lotion on her scalp until it gleamed.

"You look crazy," he said.

"You'd still get with me though."

"Yeah right. You crazy," he said again.

"Pregnant," she said to her reflection, as if it were still occurring to her, as if she wanted to see how she might take the news.

That first month, she looked severe, a person of penance or mourning. Now, after six months, her hair had grown into a boy-length thatch. She kept it disheveled with pomade, and it was beautiful.

Elsie had the kind of beauty that arrives not all at once but in a long series of moments. Micah had to learn to see it, to recognize it, and then it was all he could see and he saw it increasingly and he wished he had never learned to see it in the first place. She had deep-set eyes that lingered on everything with a look of insinuation. When she walked she always did so quickly, a slight stomp in her heels, as if with disdain for the ground itself. Her skin was light brown and moted with dark freckles across the top of her cheeks and nose. Her nose was broad and roman with a subtle aquiline bulb in its arch as if it had once been broken and by being broken somehow improved. He felt the rising of some unspoken craving looking at her face. It swung inside him like a heavy pendulum, determined, flexing slowness as a kind of power.

He ran up on the porch out of the rain, and she was there, sitting with her back against the side of the house, her belly lying loudly on top of her crossed legs. He'd been almost a mile from the house when the storm rolled in, and there was nowhere to go. It was like that in Columbia, the summer a season of sudden and violent storms.

Elsie lit a cigarette and slipped the lighter back into the cuff of her shorts and looked at him as he stood there dripping. He watched the smoke pour out of her mouth and shivered, waiting to see what she would say. It was always something, and he couldn't help now but linger to hear, couldn't help but wonder if he resembled his brother and if she cared any for the resemblance.

"Where you been out in this mess?"

"Putting out flyers. I got caught in it."

"No shit," she said.

He took off his shoes, tipped one over, and some water poured out of it. Then he tipped the other. He opened the front door and stuck his head in the house.

"Issah? Can you bring me a towel please!" he yelled into the dark of the house. The cold AC from the opened door washed out over his body. His skin clung tightly against his lank frame.

"Hush," Elsie snapped. "He's sleeping. He don't need to come out here. Just drip dry. You ain't that bad."

"My pants is soaked through."

"So take 'em off then."

Micah considered this for a moment and then grabbed his right thigh in both hands above his knee and ran his hands down along the pant leg. Water pooled around his foot. He did the other leg.

"He knows you smoke," he said.

"I know he knows."

"Then why you even care?"

"'Cause it ain't good when he's sitting here all staring at me."

"Is he really sleeping?"

"He was."

Elsie stood slowly, patting her large stomach as if she had eaten a big meal. She handed him her cigarette and went inside, the powerful hips pumping mechanically. She came out a few seconds later with a towel and laid it over his head and then took her cigarette back from between his fingers.

The towel was cinched up high around his waist and he started to work his pants off from underneath. He stepped out of them, took off his shirt, and then kicked the whole sopping pile beside the door. As he kicked the clothes a bolt of lightning landed somewhere behind their house so that the sound and the light were seamlessly bound together. The porch boards vibrated between his toes. He felt the hair on his skin rise.

"That was right there. Good lord," he said.

He hung his head around the corner of the porch and looked into the backyard to see if any of the trees were smoking when his towel suddenly disappeared from around his waist. He started for the door, but Elsie had beat him to it. He heard the deadbolt set.

"Elsie, come on now."

Through the closed door came the sound of her hissing laugh, her tongue behind her teeth. He looked up and down the street and started to fumble for his clothing. He had turned his back to the door and was trying to get his wet pants on when it opened suddenly behind him. He nearly fell into the house. Elsie was holding the towel out.

"Quit playing," he said. He stepped in the house and reached for the towel, and she backed away. The pants were wadded in one hand at his crotch. He shut the door quickly behind him.

"Quit playing. There was a car coming."

"Oh, there was a car coming? Oh no."

"Give me that towel. Please, Elsie."

"Hand me those pants and I'll put them in the wash."

He reached out for the towel. She backed away again.

"Elsie quit playing."

"Hand me those pants."

Reluctantly he gave her the pants, removed his hands from his crotch, and stood plainly before her. Elsie took a step toward him. The lights in the house flickered, and the two bodies disappeared and reappeared again, closer now. She opened the towel and walked forward with it in both hands like a mother. She moved in close and wrapped it around his waist, bringing her head under his chin and pressing her body against his. Micah grabbed the towel and turned from her and strode quickly down the narrow hallway.

"You ain't right, you know that?" he yelled.

Issah came out of his bedroom in time to collide with his younger brother.

"Micah, what the hell?" Issah yelled.

Micah was about to say something when his wet clothing hit him in the back of the head and slopped to the floor.

"Don't leave your wet clothes lying on my floor," Elsie yelled.

He reached down and picked them up without speaking and stepped past his brother into the bathroom. He closed the door and stood shivering, his heart lopping strangely in his chest. A motor missing a stroke.

"You get them flyers out today?" his brother asked through the door.

Micah didn't answer. He heard his brother move off, settle onto the living-room sofa, the TV hissing between channels. He sat down on the edge of the tub and brushed the dirt from the bottom of his feet and ran his hand under the water. When it turned warm he flipped the shower on and sat down in the tub.

His feet and legs ached. He had walked all day, doubling back through neighborhoods, doing promotion for an event that weekend at his brother's church, part of his boarding fee until he got back on his feet. His brother was one of several pastors at Kingdom Reapers Church of Salvation.

He stuffed every mailbox he passed, pulling the slips of paper from a bundle he cradled in his left arm. No one was out. Summer in Columbia and the whole city was insulated, sealed away—air-conditioning units droning in the side yards, shades drawn. Even the dogs were dispassionate, lying or stalking slowly behind their chain-link fences like zoo animals. By ten that morning the air over the asphalt was comburent like fumes, quilted with heat. He wondered how far he'd go or if he would find a place to stop midday when it got worse, worse being something he couldn't quite imagine.

His truck had never had working AC, but still he missed it. He'd been out of work for almost a year when his oil pump failed and the engine seized. He was working for a fencing company before that. They lost all of their contracts over the course of six months and the owner let everyone go, sold the equipment for scrap. After that there were no jobs; everyone was out look-ing. Micah made his living that year reclaiming used shipping pallets from distribution centers, stacking them twenty high and two deep on the back of his truck, tying them down with cable and hauling them thirty miles up 77 to a recycling center and getting $1.60 each. If he could find enough pallets to make two trips a day he did all right; more often he was lucky to get enough to make one trip. It seemed everyone was looking for the loopholes. He would arrive earlier and earlier at his normal sweet spots only to find the loading docks bare, the pallets gone, tire treads circling in the soft dirt where others before him had come away empty-handed. Then the truck broke down.

He put his last two hundred dollars into the parts and spent three days working on it. When he took it out for the first time to make a run for pallets, he found a crack in the water jacket. It was done. He got 150 dollars for scrap and it was just one more thing in a long line of things he never imagined for him-self, a life that was more desperate than he thought possible.

He came from a line of men who held odd jobs, tried entrepreneurial ventures. Micah's father had been a professional bowler after his barbershop went under. They moved to Columbia from Memphis the year Micah turned four. When his father wasn't out on the bowling circuit, he had a side business pressure washing eighteen-wheelers at truck stops. Micah could remember as a boy how his father's hands always smelled faintly of bleach. He had vitiligo on his hands, up to the wrist, and it was easy to imagine that the bleach in the water had caused his color to wash out.

His father sometimes explained his hands by screaming suddenly, and in terror, as if he hadn't noticed them before, that he had a white man's hands. He would chase his two boys around the house. *White hands is gonna get you. White hands is gonna get you.*

When Micah was old enough, he asked seriously about his father's hands and how they came to be that way. Did he get burned or something?

"Well, what's the book say?"

Micah knew he had heard this one before.

"In my mother's womb," Micah said.

"'For thou didst form my inward parts: Thou didst form me in my mother's womb.'"

His father would exclaim this with a gesture he often made, holding his hand on his chest over his heart as if the words were an oath.

"So, who it was gave me white hands?"

Micah didn't answer but watched his father's eyes buzz; he seemed wild in these moments, a man in the midst of strange incantations.

"What I asked you?"

"God did," the boy said.

"That's right. God did."

He extended his right hand, and they both looked into it as if it were a miracle, a mark of some divine visitation.

"'I am fearfully and wonderfully made: marvelous are thy works; and that my soul knoweth right well.' Now you say it. 'I am fearfully and wonderfully made.'"

"I am fearfully and wonderfully made."

"And 'Amen.'"

"Amen," Micah repeated.

But had they even been praying? His father had a way of always blurring the lines. Prayer and life, speech and creed, all netted together, on each other like lovers. His father could say *Amen* after anything and stir the colloid of his mind until everything was homily—he remembered hearing "Amen" after a strike at the bowling alley, and when his mother left them the first time, and once when his father chopped off a copperhead's head with the blade of a shovel, the snake lying in the shade under a piece of plywood the dog had been sleeping on. . . . Was everything the tail end of a sermon, an epiphanic thunderclap to parse the unparsable world, to hush the unhushable babies?

He sat down in the tub, the muscles in his feet and legs sore. He saw himself standing naked before Elsie in the living room. He could feel her heavy belly pressed against him as she wrapped the towel around his waist, could feel the heat of her skin.

Lord, he thought, and shivered.

He opened his eyes and tried to focus on something, anything, the drain, the strange patterns of rust around the chrome like the intricate, colorful patterns inside broken stone. He took some warm water in his mouth and spit it out.

He was drying when the power dropped, a deep concussion and the bathroom went dark save some weak light that fell through the hopper window and the transom. The rain was louder now with the window units not running, and it eased his mind. He listened to the different pitches of the roof gutters ringing dully, the hiss of water breaking into mist in the leaves of the large holly that overgrew their house.

When he opened the bathroom door, he saw Elsie sitting at the kitchen table with a candle burning in front of her, a fan made from a paper plate strobing between her and the candle so that her face seemed a projection, an image broken by the slowest frame rate. He turned and ducked quickly into the alcove and lay across the mattress on his back, already sweating.

The room his brother made for him was a small office alcove with two bedsheets hanging across the entrance. When he showed up two months before, the alcove contained an old desktop computer and piles of Elsie's clothes. All that stuff was still here, trapped between the wall and the bed. The only standing room was a few feet between the end of the bed and the sheet curtains.

The smallness of the space wasn't discomforting. A bed under a roof was all that mattered now. He knew many people who were on the streets after the recession, who had no family. He liked the cramped feeling of this space, the feeling of being stashed away somewhere obscure. He rolled over and was drifting off when his brother stuck his head in between the sheets.

"You had anything to eat yet?"

"No. But I'm hungry."

"We can't make anything till the power comes back on."

"All right."

"You want to walk down to Edna's for us?"

"Will she have power?"

"She don't need it to sell what she already has. Power just went out."

"All right."

He pulled on his only pair of dry pants and a gray T-shirt and headed for the door. The rain was just a mist now, and the massive, slow drops from the trees fell heavily on his shoulders and in the puddles of the street. Hailstones gleamed in the grass like pearls. When he appeared at Edna's stand, he saw through the one sliding window a flashlight whisking around frenetically. He knocked on the window and heard the door around back quickly shut and lock.

"Edna, you open?" he asked, rapping his knuckles on the glass.

"One sec now, sugar." And again the flashlight swung, accompanied by the sound of ice being poured into coolers.

"Okay, what can I do for you, baby? We don't have much. I'm 'bout to lose all my meat if they don't get this power back on, and they ain't gonna replace it. Hell no. Say I'm suppose to have a generator anyway." She was laughing now, always laughing.

"What's not cold yet?"

"Well, it's all cold, sugar. I got some fries and hotdogs."

"All right then."

Edna gave him a brown paper bag, and then she took some time thinking about how much to charge him for the cold food.

"Just give me four dollars," she said.

Micah handed her the ten-dollar bill his brother gave him. She handed him back his change and told him to be good.

"You know I will."

"All right now," she said, laughing.

A cop had been called into the small white section of the neighborhood to cruise, its searchlights trolling out in every direction, bright as lightning. It gave the impression that it was scraping the remnant light from the surface of the world, pushing it out in front of itself like a bulldozer. Gentrification. He had heard the word at the gas station the week before and knew what it meant without having to ask. Young white families in the North Main area with children in expensive-looking strollers, rescued Labs trotting alongside. Rent would go up. That's what it meant. The alarm systems were down and the people who had them were calling the cops in after the big storms—fanciful imaginations, expecting what exactly? Riots?

The cop turned, came back toward Micah, and slowed to a crawl alongside him. Micah didn't look at the car, kept walking. He could hear the valves of the engine sucking, the compressor clicking on and off.

"Where you headed tonight, buddy?" The voice came out from the dark interior where a screen was casting blue digital light on a pale fresh face. He put a flashlight in Micah's face and then turned it off.

"Home."

"You live this way?"

"About a block this way, yeah."

"You sure?"

"I'm staying with my brother and his wife. 3012."

The officer looked up the street and then back at Micah. Micah stopped walking, and the officer put the car in park.

"What's in that bag there?"

Micah felt a shard of anger flare up hard. He looked up the street toward his brother's house. Suddenly, it was impossibly far. No one else was out walking. Just him and this cop, and that was all. He shook his head in disbelief. This is happening, he told himself.

"Hot dogs," he said.

"There ain't an open container in that bag, is there?"

"I just said it's hot dogs."

The cop checked his rearview window and then put the flashlight in Micah's eyes again.

"You mind if I have a look?"

Micah wiped his face. He could let this go. You can, he thought. He wondered how old the cop was, where he went to high school.

"You want to look at my hot dogs?"

"Is that a problem?"

The cop was on his radio now. Another man's voice sizzled. A number was spat out and Micah knew a number like that could sum him up if he would give this man the excuse. He turned the bag over and dumped it out on the sidewalk. He shook it empty and showed the cop the empty bag. He crumpled the bag up, as if even an *empty* bag could get him in trouble. The hot dogs looked a strange green color against the wet concrete.

"You didn't need to spoil your dinner, son."

"It was already spoiled," Micah said.

"You mind picking that up?" The cop put the cruiser in drive and headed slowly up the road, the lights incising the world before him, leaving everything behind in darkness. When the cruiser turned the corner, Micah nudged the food into the street gutter with his shoe and tossed the bag into the tall grass. He thought about going back to Edna's to buy more food but could not bring himself to turn around. He put his hands in his pockets and strolled on the quiet dark street. *Fearfully and wonderfully made*, he thought to himself, *to be made in fear and so to live in fear—how is such a thing to ever be considered wonderful?*

"Where's the food?" his brother asked, turning his chair from the table to face Micah as he came down the hallway. Issah had his wave cap on, and he looked mean, ready for something to get him going.

"The bag broke," Micah said.

"The bag broke?"

"Yeah."

"Was you holding it from the bottom?"

"I wasn't planning on having it break."

They sat in the kitchen eating cold canned soup and pieces of sandwich bread in the candlelight. Elsie was reading a magazine up close to her face, and his brother was throwing open cabinets and slamming them shut again.

"There's nothing else."

"I know it," he said.

"You should go to bed anyway," she said.

"I ain't preaching tomorrow," he said, sitting back down at the table.

"Who is?" she asked.

"Randy Miller."

"Who's doing Sunday school?"

"I guess we ain't having it."

"I could watch smoke forever," Micah said, as if no one had been speaking. He stared into the apex of the flame.

Elsie and Issah looked at him.

"I bet you could too, you freak."

"Elsie, shut it," Issah said.

"What is smoke anyway?" Micah asked.

"Jesus. What is smoke? What do you mean, what is smoke? Smoke is smoke."

"Don't say that," Issah said.

"Say what?" she asked.

"Don't say *Jesus* like that."

"I'm not doing this," Elsie said.

She blew out the candle, went into the bedroom, and left the two brothers sitting together in the dark. They listened as she closed and opened the closet doors and then they heard the bed creaking and settling.

"Make a beat," Issah said.

Micah started drumming on the table, then his brother started filling it in, syncopating out sections with his knuckles against the wood. It rose up into a clatter.

"Will y'all shut up?" Elsie screamed from the bedroom, and the two brothers laughed, stood, and put their plates into the sink. The rain had calmed, and the house seemed to fill with silence so complete it felt like it weighed something. There was no traffic on the street. No dogs could be heard barking in the adjoining yards. They said goodnight to each other in the silence. Issah hit his younger brother in the shoulder as he turned, and in the dark hall Micah imagined the expression on his brother's face, the easy smile that had always been a comfort, a sign of stability he had learned to trust. It would all be all right. He'd get it back. He'd be all right.

In the middle of the night the power came on and woke him. Beneath his back, the sheet was damp with sweat. He got up to pee, turning off the lights in the hallway as he went. The TV in the living room was on, a loud growl of static. The overhead fan felt marvelous. He lay down on the sofa and let the fan wash air over his slick skin. Relief from the heat was lulling him to sleep again when he saw the front door open, a tiny slat of blue growing into a band. Elsie's round figure stepped into the gap and out onto the porch while the door eased carefully shut behind her. He saw the wavering of a lighter through the window and the silhouette from the street lights against the blinds and watched her shadow pace.

He woke with her easing down beside him on the sofa, the smell of cigarette smoke and lotion strong in her hair.

She swung a leg up over his stomach, and her large belly felt tight as a drum against his chest.

"Elsie?" he said weakly.

"You feel like ice, boy. You feel good."

She slid herself down along his body so that her face was near his.

"Elsie, what are you doing?"

She did not answer but put her face firmly against his and left it there, the heat dissipating out of her cheek. It seemed an hour passed this way, though it could only have been a minute, and Micah's mind was racing, his hands limp at his side. She turned her lips against his neck and kissed him softly.

"What was you saying?" she asked.

"You need to go to bed."

He found the words heavy. He could feel the weight of her breasts, swollen against his chest, a throbbing between his legs.

"It's hot as shit in there," she said, whispering now.

He tried again to speak but could not. He found his hand moving up the outside of her leg and then his fingers inside the cuff of her boxer shorts. Her legs were strong, the muscles pronounced. He could taste the salt of sweat on her lips. He was swinging over something very deep, swinging out again and again, feeling the endlessness appearing and then disappearing under him. He thought about the cop, the imbalance of everything he had ever known, the confluence of it, the fires he had seen in his life. Why did he think about these things? He thought about the fact that he had never stolen a single thing; not once in his life had he taken something that wasn't his. Oh God, he thought, dear God.

Elsie pulled off her shirt and let her weight settle into him. She began to grapple with his clothing. He felt the hot skin of her arms giving between his fingers, felt the spring of her ribs, the notches of her backbone. He ran his fingers over her belly and down between her legs.

The need to be quiet, to be absolutely quiet, made each move excruciating. It came over them both at the same moment and they focused entirely on it. The silence consumed them, swallowed them, minute by minute, as if it were a depth they were plunging farther into. And then, before he knew what was happening or that it was over, she was standing over him with her clothing crumpled in her hand, not looking back at him as she turned and went into the bathroom. He was alone, and he thought for a moment it had all been a dream he had just woken from.

—

When he got up from the sofa, it was very early, and he wasn't sure if he had slept or just lain there all night, remote from himself. Twice, as he tried to sleep, he went into the bathroom and vomited, avoiding the mirror lest he catch a glimpse of himself. It had not been a dream; the smell of her lotion coated his hands, his face. He washed. His stomach had turned into acid and his heart ran high and then it plummeted and when it was high he was full of panic and when it ran low he was a shell. He would drift off slowly until a sense of fear and lustiness overtook him and he would walk again quickly to the bathroom to be sick. But now the feeling wasn't of sickness or panic but of something else, the anticipation of movement, the need to get out of there.

He went into his room and put on his clothes and threw some more clothing into a backpack he found beneath the desk. He went into the kitchen, lifted his brother's wallet from the table and took out all the cash inside. He stuffed the bills into his pants pocket and was soon on the porch, putting his feet into the damp shoes, easing the door closed behind him. He needed to walk, to keep himself moving. This was right, he thought. This is all there is.

—

At the Greyhound station several men were standing around a teller booth looking at departure times and talking with one another. It seemed that these men had not slept, that they were still in the midst of their rambles, mourning their various losses. They smelled heavy of alcohol and urine. He moved past them and saw the time for Atlanta and knew it was soon enough to get him gone, and he waited for the teller's attention and when he got it spoke the words—Atlanta, one way—listening to the sound of his voice passing into the speak-through grill and then resonating with a metallic one-dimensional note inside where the man sat. Suddenly he was in the yard of their first home, he and his brother; a large coffee can was up to his face, and inside the can was a knot and from the knot came a brittle version of his brother's voice singing, "Let the stew of heaven fall upon my thirsty soul, let the stew of heaven fall on me," over and over again.

It had been a Sunday afternoon, warm in the early spring, and his brother had been changing the words to the hymn they sang that morning. His brother's laughter was like bands of wind shivering on a body of water. The feeling inside him was airy and free. He could see the wrinkles beside his brother's eyes, could see the greatness of his brother, and it woke a horrible fear. This thing, it will never be undone, forever and ever done.

He thought of that same afternoon with his brother after church and the strange turn it took. They had taken a can of WD-40 and a lighter from the garage and burned the tent-caterpillar nests that hung low in boughs of the crape myrtles in their side yard. They sprayed the oil from the can with the lighter extended, a makeshift blowtorch. They let the smoking arcs of greasy fire fall on the nests and watched as the caterpillars burned and dripped into the grass. Was this a wicked thing? He remembered it; he remembered the whistling sound. He remembered telling himself it was not the caterpillars making that strange noise.

He could see his life now strung along, a series of choices that were not strong, a failure of heart at every turn, a giving way to something in himself he did not love. Each thing seemed tributary to this final thing, to the way he held Elsie in the silence they kept together and the horrible shudder he felt inside his body when he finished with her against him. Nothing would change these facts, but he found a relief in knowing that he could call himself loathsome and it be true. He could see himself clearly now, a confused thing, a muddled thing. All his life, he was only that. That was his truth, and he knew somehow that he could leverage it, that it was powerful, and rare. If there was to be something other than fear, if he was to be wonderful, it could only be on the other side of this truth. He could start over now, just him and the terrible truth.

He counted out the money now, forty-two dollars. He passed two twenty-dollar bills beneath the plexiglass and took his ticket. He would start over with nothing, like he needed to.

Several men were sleeping outside along the edge of a low concrete wall. They did not notice him as he walked past and lay down beside them. He lay as they did, his face turned into the shrinking piece of shade; he lay and for an hour listened for the sound of the big diesel to come into the lot to take him off.

In that long hour he saw his brother and Elsie sitting in the folding chairs in the little worship hall of their church building, saw the collection plate going round and round again, his brother counting the money and stuffing it into his pockets, his brother putting his arm around the back of his wife's chair, fanning himself with his hat. He heard the music, the songs, the stomping of feet.

"Where is Micah this morning?" his brother asked.

"Do I look like his babysitter?" Elsie said.

The deacons had bright-colored handkerchiefs that matched their bright-colored ties, gold, messianic purple, blue, and they passed them quickly under the brims of their hats and returned them to their coat pockets. And then there was the reverend, Randy Miller, out back of the building, pacing in the unmowed centipede grass, begging for the right words, begging for the Spirit.

Acknowledgments

The author gratefully acknowledges the editors of the following publications where some of these stories first appeared in slightly different form: *Narrative Magazine* ("The Strength of Fields," "Stretch Out Your Hand," and "Silas"); *Image* ("A Map of the Watershed"); *The Chattahoochee Review* ("Father Brother Keeper"); *The Four Way Review* ("Lipochrome") *Pacifica Literary Review* ("They Were Calling to One Another"); *Nat. Brut.* ("Swing Low Sweet Chicken Baby").

Thank you to the Milton Center at *Image* and Warren Wilson College for generous fellowships that allowed me time to work at crucial moments in the life of this book.

Thank you to Genesis Chapman for the use of his painting for the cover.

The title "The Strength of Fields" is taken from a poem of the same title by James Dickey. The phrase "wild to be wreckage forever" is from Dickey's poem "Cherrylog Road." The phrase "the wide and single stars" is from John Berryman's poem "Eleven Addresses to Our Lord." The phrase "swallowed like spent stars against the dark vault" is from Sean Nevin's "Losing Solomon."

I am indebted to so many gifted teachers, readers, mentors, and friends: Megan Staffel, Robert Boswell, Maud Casey,

Dominic Smith, Shann Ray, Matt Roesch, Jane Rose Porter, Geeta Kothari, Olga Zilberbourg, Tom Jenks, Paul Bowers, Gregory Wolfe, Mary Kenagy Mitchell, and Ben Greer; the entire community of Warren Wilson's MFA program, with special thanks to Debra Allbery and Ellen Bryant Voigt for their guidance and encouragement; Claudia Ballard, for reading this book a hundred times and still believing in it. Thank you all.

Special thanks to Kirby Gann, Sarah Gorham, and the rest of Sarabande for their excellence, patience, and tremendous care.

I am profoundly grateful to my community and family in South Carolina and abroad who offer me unmerited member-ship and encouragement. Thank you, Lydia, for being at the center of that membership, for your grace and love, for the life you share with me.

Note on the Cover Artist:
Genesis Chapman grew up in Bent Mountain, Virginia. For nearly a decade he has investigated what he calls the *genus loci* of Bent Mountain, distilling the emotions associated with his long-standing love of that place into sinuous, elemental forms. The cover painting, "Spring 2010, Bottom Creek, Bent Mountain, Ink on Yupo Paper," is originally 15 x 8 ft. Find more of his work at www.genesischapman.com.

Josh Rainwater

NATHAN POOLE received the 2012 *Narrative* Prize and served as the Milton Postgraduate Fellow in Writing at *Image* during the 2013–14 academic year, and is the Joan Beebe fellow at Warren Wilson College. He considers himself an amateur dendrologist and theologian, and has worked as a carpenter and plumber most of his adult life. His stories have appeared in a number of journals, including *The Kenyon Review, Narrative Magazine, The Chattahoochie Review, Image, Nat.Brut., The Lumière Reader, Strangers Magazine, The Drum Literary Magazine, Pacifica Literary Review, The Four Way Review,* and *The Saturday Evening Post.* In 2014 an expanded version of "The Firelighter" won the *Quarterly West* Novella Contest.

Sarabande Books thanks you for the purchase of this book; we do hope you enjoy it! Founded in 1994 as an independent, nonprofit, literary press, Sarabande publishes poetry, short fiction, and literary nonfiction—genres increasingly neglected by commercial publishers. We are committed to producing beautiful, lasting editions that honor exceptional writing, and to keeping those books in print. If you're interested in further reading, take a moment to browse our website, www. sarabandebooks.org. There you'll find information about other titles; opportunities to contribute to the Sarabande mission; and an abundance of supporting materials including audio, video, a lively blog, and our Sarabande in Education program.